MOJITO & LOVE
Christine Krause

About the author

Christine Krause writes feel-good contemporary romance novels. Born and raised in the Ruhrgebiet in Germany, Christine moved to Canada when she was seventeen to attend University in Nova Scotia. She later graduated with her Ph.D. in History from Carleton University in 2019. After meeting her husband during a semester abroad at a Canadian high school, it seemed fated that she either become a screenwriter for a teen movie or write romantic comedies.

Christine currently lives on a small farm in Ontario, Canada with her beautiful daughter and husband. When not writing or teaching, Christine can usually be found playing with her toddler or riding one of her four horses.

Mojito & Love

CHRISTINE KRAUSE

ISBN: 978-1-990703-05-8

Editing Services by V. Clifton

For my family.
Danke!

PROLOGUE

Walking down the aisle of the supermarket with its unfamiliar labels, Lanie felt no remnants of the determination that had gotten her through the past twenty-four hours. There was only so much energy to get a person through, and hers was simply used up.

After leaving the plane, her stomach had been growling loud enough that she couldn't ignore it any longer. Given her limited funds, she'd headed to the small supermarket near the main street of Bocas, only a ten-minute walk from the small airport on Colón Island where she'd landed, rather than indulging in a warm meal at one of the restaurants that lined the waterfront.

Of course, after she got through here, she might have some bread and cheese to soothe the emptiness of her stomach, but she'd still be in a new place without a clue where she would sleep tonight.

Right now, standing in this aisle filled with all sorts of brand products she wasn't used to, she was fairly certain she'd reached the limit of what she could withstand. It had been her choice to leave, but in this moment, she'd give anything to return to her apartment where her comfortable bed stood empty and unused.

She leaned against the shelf, clutching her over-sized purse. She didn't allow herself to close her eyes, unwilling to lose sight of the second bag she had stored in the small grocery cart. A tear ran down her cheek, and she quickly wiped it away. She couldn't break down yet. Not when she still had to figure out where she was going next.

"Are you all right?" A short older woman with ample curves gave her a once-over. She looked to be somewhere in her early sixties and seemed used to having people answer to her. With her hands on her round waist, Lanie had the impression that this woman wasn't concerned as much as she was judging her.

"Uh, yes, I'm fine. Thank you." Apparently, she looked as rundown as she felt. Lovely.

"And you expect me to believe that?" The *humpf* noise the woman made would have been comical if Lanie had energy to spare for humor.

"I'll be fine, but thank you for checking on me." She tried to turn away, but the woman stopped her with a firm hand on her arm.

Inspecting Lanie's shopping cart, the woman announced, "You need some juice, not water. Come with me." The woman took Lanie's hand and pulled her back to the aisle with the drinks. Lanie just grabbed hold of her cart, pulling it behind them, too surprised to argue.

Grabbing a carton of orange juice, the stranger turned back to Lanie. "Here, this has some sugar and calories so you won't faint on the way to your hotel."

Given that the woman didn't look like she was willing to accept any backtalk, and the fact that she was probably right about Lanie needing the sugar to get through the rest of the day, Lanie nodded and accepted the juice.

When the woman walked off, Lanie grabbed a pack of granola bars and went to the front to pay. She could always come back tomorrow.

Loading the few items she'd picked up on the little conveyor belt, Lanie noticed that the older woman came up behind her at the cash registrar, carrying no fewer than five bags of lemons. This time, the woman didn't say a word, only watching as Lanie carefully pulled out the right number of coins. After handing the cashier the money she owed, she stepped back out onto the dusty side road, relieved to no longer be under someone's scrutiny no matter how kind the stranger had been.

Before everything had started, she'd probably have asked the woman about those lemons. Perhaps she was planning on making fresh lemonade for her grandchildren? But today, or rather in the past year, her desire to talk with strangers had become less and less. And wasn't that just sad?

Standing in the hot afternoon sun, wearing her travel clothes and holding on to two bags and the groceries, Lanie almost let herself sink to the ground. The past couple of months since her best friend had fled, leaving Lanie to deal with the fallout, had been enough to wear her down, but until now, she hadn't allowed it to break her. Now, though, with sweat pouring down her neck and left with none of the security her old life had given her, she wasn't so sure she could take even one more step.

Except her old life wasn't safe anymore either, so she had no other choice.

Lanie turned to the waterfront. She wouldn't be able to afford a hotel for more than a couple of nights, but tonight, she'd bite the bullet and pay whatever she had to in order to get a good night's sleep. Tomorrow, she could figure out what she would do next.

"Which hotel are you staying in?" The familiar voice came from behind her, and Lanie cringed at the unexpected closeness of another person.

"Jumpy, aren't you?"

When Lanie turned to face the older woman this time, she already expected the scrutinizing expression on her face.

"Just tired," she lied, trying to gather her thoughts. It would do her no good to keep evading. Since this woman was obviously a local, she might as well take advantage of the opportunity. "I didn't book anything, but I'm hoping to find a room for tonight."

It was already four in the afternoon, but since this was a place that lived on tourism, Lanie figured there would have to be free rooms around. "Is there a place you know of that might have a room for me and isn't too pricey?"

Instead of answering, the woman looked her over once again. "You don't look like the backpacking sort, and you're definitely not one of those fancy tourists we get. What brings you here?"

The question was intrusive, and Lanie wouldn't answer it, but somehow, the woman was endearing. As she considered what to say, Lanie returned the woman's scrutiny. Fairly short and quite curvy, the older woman was obviously fit for her age. She also looked truly interested in what Lanie was doing here, and Lanie just wasn't the kind of person to push others away. At least, she didn't use to be.

For today, she'd gone through enough, and allowing herself to be honest with another person might just help her feel a little more normal.

"I'm moving here. At least, I think I will. I'm going to need a job and a place to stay, but I guess for tonight, all I need is a bed. I've had a long day of traveling."

The woman nodded, though her eyebrows drew together disapprovingly. Just when Lanie thought she'd walk away without giving her any directions, the woman finally spoke again. "Okay then. Everyone here calls me Mama Lita, so you might as well call me that too. Come along. You look like you'll keel over if we don't get you to sit down and have some of that juice."

Twenty minutes later, Lanie sat in Mama Lita's kitchen drinking orange juice and eating a spicy dish with beans and rice. Her host had disappeared to change, leaving Lanie to wonder how she'd ended up trusting this stranger enough to come here. Despite knowing she probably should, she couldn't bring herself to regret her impulsive decision.

When Mama Lita reappeared, she was no longer wearing the casual shirt and pants from earlier but a dress with large orange flowers and green leaves printed on it. The woman was quite a colorful sight, and Lanie couldn't help but grin.

"Do you have plans tonight?"

She'd been right earlier. Just having some company and food had helped her find her equilibrium again, and it was nice to have a normal conversation. Still, she was already imposing on this stranger more than she should have. "I don't want to keep you. I really appreciate the meal, but if you're heading out, I can be on my way."

"Nonsense. You're not keeping me, otherwise I'd have sent you on your way already. When you're done eating, you can drop your bag in the spare room. Tonight, you can sleep there. Then get yourself freshened up. We have to leave soon."

Lanie stared at the woman. Before everything with Collin, she'd been as easygoing and trusting with strangers as Mama Lita seemed to be, but by now, she'd learned that there was a good reason to be careful.

"That's so nice of you, and I really appreciate the offer, but are you sure? You don't even know me. I'm okay with taking a hotel."

Mama Lita let out another *humpf.* "If you do anything but pass out tonight, I'd be surprised, so I'm not taking much of a risk."

It wasn't exactly a compliment or an expression of trust, but Lanie's current appearance probably warranted the statement. And despite her own assurance that she could get a hotel room, she truly didn't have a ton of money to spare. Unable to use her credit cards, she had taken whatever cash she and her parents had on hand, but after the plane tickets, there wasn't much left. A free place to sleep would actually be great, so she nodded, hoping Mama Lita could see how grateful she was.

Once she found a job, she'd repay the woman's kindness in whatever way she would permit, though Lanie got the impression that Mama Lita would refuse to accept anything that would seem like she was being compensated for her help. Despite the intrusive and brisk way the woman had about her, Lanie could tell she was as kind as they came.

Then something Mama Lita had said occurred to Lanie. "Wait, did you say we were going somewhere?"

"If you want a job, then yes."

Before Lanie could decide whether this was the best luck she'd had in years or simply a terrible idea, she was following Mama Lita down Bocas's main street and into a small boat. A short boat ride later, during which Lanie got to admire the beautiful Caribbean beaches for the very first time in her life, they arrived at a small pier that looked much newer than the one they'd used in Bocas.

Before taking the hand the water cab driver offered Mama Lita, the woman handed Lanie the large grocery bag full of lemons she'd brought with her. If her life hadn't been so utterly awful lately, Lanie would have laughed at the irony. When life gave you lemons...

"Why are you dragging a bag full of lemons with you, anyway?" Why it only occurred to her now to ask this question, Lanie wasn't sure. Probably because at this point in her life, it was just easier to simply go with the strange things that were happening around her than to keep questioning everything. How else was she supposed to hang on to the remnants of her sanity?

"Oh, those are for the wedding."

"Wait, you're taking me to a wedding?"

Whether it was the shock in her expression or the idea that she was worried about crashing a wedding, Lanie didn't know, but instead of taking her concern seriously, Mama Lita laughed. "No, I'll introduce you to the manager so you can interview. Then you go home, and I go to the wedding. My niece and I will come home later, and we can speak tomorrow."

Lanie supposed she should be grateful. Earlier, she hadn't known where she'd spend the night and what she'd do the next day, and now she was apparently heading to a job interview. If she still believed in fairy tales, Lanie would think Mama Lita was her fairy godmother.

Moments later, when Mama Lita had shown her to a bench outside what looked to be the reception building of the resort, the idea that she'd ended up in a weird modern version of a fairy tale seemed even more likely.

This place was beautiful.

Lanie had never been to the Caribbean before, and after the boat ride over the glistening blue water, seeing the white beaches in the evening sun, and now sitting surrounded by lush green vegetation with birds singing all around her, it was difficult not to feel as if magic had come to save her from what she'd feared would be her exile. She never used to be a pessimist, and this gorgeous place seemed like a sign from the universe that she shouldn't give up just yet.

As Mama Lita left her sitting in what she'd called the welcome center of the resort, Lanie knew one thing. She'd say whatever she needed to get the job that Mama Lita had brought her here for.

When she heard the low humming of an electric engine, she looked up and saw Mama Lita steering the golf cart she'd taken off in earlier toward the welcome center. Next to her fairy godmother sat an incredibly handsome man, and Lanie had to blink because for a moment, her brain told her that this must be her fairy-tale prince. Except, when she rose to greet what must be the manager, her purse fell against her hip, reminding her of the fake papers she was using.

Maybe this was paradise and not exile, but this man couldn't be her prince.

* * *

The woman waiting for them at the welcome center looked like she'd gone through a hell of a day, and yet, she was more beautiful than any of the women at his best friend's wedding reception that Mama Lita had dragged him away from.

Mama Lita was one of the very few people who never asked for anything from him, which was why he'd agreed to leave Logan's and Jane's celebration to conduct a job interview despite never having advertised an open position. It wasn't as if the resort couldn't use more staff, so here he was, wearing his best man's suit, ready to find out what the unconventional appearance of the woman was all about.

Her coloring was lighter than his own, making her stand apart from the locals. As Mama Lita parked the golf cart she'd brought to pick him up in, the woman watched him with wide doe-like eyes. He would have liked to think his appearance was so captivating that she couldn't blink, but the way she held herself suggested she was more closely mimicking the stereotypical deer in the headlights.

She'd been holding her hands in her lap when they first arrived, as if comforting herself, and now that she stood to greet them, she was clutching the oversized purse that was strung over her shoulder as if it represented her lifeline. He supressed the urge to reach out and gently pry her hands free.

Despite her somewhat dishevelled appearance, she was very attractive, which was a good reminder of why this was probably a terrible idea. He'd had a few glasses of champagne after the ceremony, and here he was, looking at her and wondering whether he should invite her back to the wedding and dance with her so she'd feel less anxious rather than acting like a professional should. Like a potential boss should.

Oblivious to his thoughts, Mama Lita gestured at the woman and introduced her in English. "Jordan, this is Lanie."

Pushing her shoulders back, the woman stepped forward. "Hello, it's nice to meet you." She spoke in fluent Spanish, though with an accent.

"It's nice to meet you as well, Lanie. I'm Jordan, the resort manager. How about we go into my office?"

"I'll send someone to take you home later," Mama Lita declared before turning around and heading for the golf cart, obviously intent on joining the wedding festivities.

He led Lanie into his office, where they sat facing each other across the desk.

"You speak English and Spanish?"

"I do, yes." They switched to English now, with Lanie adjusting easily into what he thought sounded like an American accent, perhaps from Maine, though he couldn't be too sure. They had many people from the States visit the resort each year, giving Jordan the chance to listen to a variety of different accents, but he'd never been great at distinguishing the regional differences.

"Do you have any experience in the hospitality industry?"

She hesitated slightly before answering. "No, actually, I don't. I have no job references either, but Mama Lita mentioned that there might be something available. I'm happy to do whatever is needed."

Her honesty surprised him. For obvious reasons, people often preferred to start with flattering descriptions of their work ethic and experience. He considered for a moment. "Well, we do need more cleaning staff. If you have no references, one of those positions could be a fit for you." He left the statement hanging in the air, curious how she'd react to the offer.

"That would be great."

The relief he saw in her eyes made him wonder what this woman had gone through to end up here in the late evening without references. "You know, with your being bilingual, you might find a better paying position in Bocas Town." He wasn't sure why he said it, but he couldn't help himself. Something about her made him want to help her. Or maybe it was a selfish impulse to keep temptation away from himself.

"Oh, no, I'd like to take the cleaning job if I can start right away." She looked exhausted and defeated, but it was obvious that she was serious. She wanted to have this job, perhaps needed it, and Jordan couldn't bring himself to take the hope he saw in her tired face away from her.

"You'll be on a probationary period for the first three months. During that time, we can terminate your employment immediately. After that, you'll have the same contract as the rest of the staff."

He explained the contract briefly before handing her a copy and the paperwork she needed to fill out. "Fill this out and bring it in on Monday. If I'm not here, just drop it on my desk. I have some meetings in the morning, so I might be out of the office. I'll contact you if there are any problems. Someone will meet you and point out the schedule to you. They'll also show you where you can grab a uniform that fits."

Surprise registered on her face. "So, I have the job?"

He nodded, and her expression shifted into a genuine smile. "Thank you."

Her words sounded as if she wasn't quite able to believe her luck, and her obvious elation tugged at something in him.

Before he could say something else, someone knocked at the door. "Mama Lita send me to take Lanie home?"

Lanie stood, still smiling. "Thank you, Jordan. I promise I'll do excellent work, and you won't even notice I'm here."

As she left his office, Jordan watched. Somehow, he doubted he'd ever *not* notice when she was around.

CHAPTER 1

Scrubbing the countertop of the Caribbean villa, Lanie had to smile. She'd hardly dreamed of being a cleaning lady one day, but it could've been worse.

Her eyes wandered from the now clean surface to the glass double-doors that were still covered with handprints and fingerprints where the last renters had pushed the doors open. She could see over the canopy of palm trees right to the ocean. Even after a month of working at the Howler Island resort, she still couldn't get enough of that view, so different from where she'd lived in the city.

The steep hill going down toward the water that made it possible to see the ocean from all the villas of the resort made her morning walks a lot more challenging than she'd anticipated, but she enjoyed the exercise and her body was already growing stronger.

The job was also surprisingly not that bad. Before all this, she'd imagined a cleaning position to involve all kinds of nasty things. Instead, most of her work was to shine up almost clean surfaces.

Of course, not everything was fun, but even the more disgusting things she had to clean rewarded her with instant gratification when she saw that she'd managed to get rid of all the grime. There was something to be said for seeing the results of your hard work right away. It was certainly very different from the long-term projects she'd worked on in her job as a marketing specialist.

Still, as she packed up her supplies, Lanie was grateful that she could use one of the resort's golf carts to get from one villa to the next. She hadn't been used to physical labor, and although she was building muscle quickly, she still felt sore each evening. Not that she'd complain.

Leaving the villa, she lifted her bucket onto the storage area of the converted golf cart and went back in to get the vacuum cleaner.

When she'd left her home a month ago, she hadn't been able to bring much. One bag full of clothes and other items that she'd needed to start over and a large purse with all the important documents she couldn't leave behind. That was all she had to her name now.

18

Fortunately, she was smart enough to know that material possessions only mattered when you had the luxury to have them. Here, she had something more important. Her sanity.

As long as she had this job and earned enough money to eat and rent a place to sleep, she'd be okay.

Better than before, anyway.

The thought of what she'd left behind still made her insides hurt, but over the past month, she'd gotten better at ignoring the feeling and focusing on the important task at hand, surviving and creating a new life for herself.

As it stood, she didn't have much of a choice anymore, anyway.

This island was the perfect place for her, and she'd been lucky to have gotten this job so quickly. The fact that she spoke Spanish had definitely helped. Despite the local dialect, the other workers understood her Spanish just fine, and thankfully, in the resort, the primary spoken language was English. It made things easy for her, though she hardly ever spoke to anyone other than Mama Lita and her niece, Gabriela.

Lanie pulled on the skirt of her uniform before sitting down behind the wheel. Even though the uniforms weren't cut all that short, the skirt did tend to hike up when she sat down, and the black bench of the golf cart was always scorching hot after sitting out in the sun.

Driving to the next villa, Lanie waived at Dr. Jane Graw, wife of one of the resort's owners and head of the local animal research facility that was located near the welcome center. They seemed to be on a similar schedule since it wasn't the first time Lanie had driven past her just as Dr. Graw was coming out of the private road that led to the owners' cottages. The woman waved back, a friendly but distracted smile on her face.

It was one of the things Lanie liked about this island. There was a welcoming but reserved atmosphere. Since the resort, with its eco-villas and the small but exclusive hotel, catered to the rich, the general attitude that was expected of the staff was a friendly but nearly invisible demeanor.

That was exactly what she needed. To stay invisible if at all possible.

Of course, in the back areas of the restaurant, welcome center, and marina, the staff was a lot more outgoing, and Lanie had quickly been accepted by the locals who worked here. She wasn't sure whether it was due to the influence of Mama Lita that she'd been so easily welcomed into the group of resort workers who, for the most part, were from around Bocas and Glamirante, the one village on the other end of the island, or whether it was simply the Caribbean way. Either way, she was grateful.

Having to deal with the scrutiny of other workers who were unhappy to see a stranger invade their home would have made her life more complicated. This way, she could more easily avoid attention.

After stopping in front of her next villa, Lanie slid her universal key card through the electronic lock. This was the last place she had on her roster for the morning, and her stomach let her know she needed to take a break afterward to eat something. It had been a constant struggle to eat enough in the past weeks, and she was trying hard to take better care of herself.

Less than five weeks ago, Mama Lita had found her in that little grocery store, and it had all worked out so well that she couldn't shake the feeling that it wouldn't be long before she'd be called back into Jordan Dane's office and find herself without a job or a home once more. She was still in the contractual trial period, so he'd be able to send her on her way with no prior warning.

Needless to say, her anxiety was killing her appetite, and that just wouldn't do.

While Lanie got to work cleaning the bathrooms of her last villa, wiping away the dirt that had collected behind the faucet, she reminded herself of how lucky she was despite the paranoia that kept trying to creep in. At least right now, she had a job and a place to live, and she was somewhere where she could remain anonymous and nobody would think twice to look for her.

"Lanie?" a voice called from the lower floor.

"I'm up here!" Lanie smiled. Well, almost no one was looking for her.

Gabriela, Mama Lita's niece and currently Lanie's housemate, came into the bathroom.

"What's up?"

"Are you almost done here?" Gabriela asked. "Jordan called a staff meeting."

Lanie's good mood dimmed a little. Jordan was the very person she tried to avoid as best as she could. She figured that *out of sight, out of mind* was her best strategy to keep her job. That and doing good work, of course.

Lying to people just didn't sit right with her, and she mainly got away with being evasive when anyone asked her something she couldn't answer, but she'd had to show Jordan her fake papers to get the job. Knowing herself, she'd blurt out just the right thing to make him realize he'd hired a fraudster. It was better if she didn't draw Jordan's attention. Then she'd be fine.

It was ironic, really. She'd spent all her training and career trying to get people to notice things. Products, companies, and even people. Now she was trying to do the exact opposite. And unfortunately, her lack of qualification in the field was becoming more and more obvious in the past weeks.

Whenever she couldn't avoid running into him, Jordan looked at her so intently, as if he considered her a puzzle he wanted to solve. So not part of her plan!

It was downright unnerving, and even though he was always polite and professional, he somehow seemed too interested in her. She'd spent more than one evening repeating one of her most used mantras to herself—*stay as far away from Jordan Dane as possible without being obvious.*

It was the very mantra she recalled to herself now. "I just started cleaning here. Do you think you can fill me in later?"

Gabriela shook her head, destroying Lanie's hope with all the nonchalance of someone who had no worries in the world. "He said he wanted everyone there. I'll just get started on the downstairs. If we work quickly, I'm sure we can get back to the center in time."

Lanie suppressed a sigh. "Okay, thank you."

Less than forty-five minutes later, Gabriela steered the golf cart into one of the parking spots and Lanie connected it to the charging station. They walked past the reception desk and into a side door that led to the large break room which simultaneously functioned as a meeting room for the resort workers.

Immediately, the cool air of the building brought her some much-needed relief from the humidity outdoors. Every day, the cleaning crew, marina staff, and admin folks all came together in the break room to get some rest and cool off from the hot and humid air outside. And on rare occasions like today, everyone gathered here for staff meetings.

Stepping into the room, the noise of conversations enveloped them.

"I'm just going to grab my lunch," Lanie told Gabriela and quickly made her way over to the lockers in the back corner of the room. She really needed to have something in her stomach, but before she could get to her lunch bag, Jordan Dane stepped into the room and the conversations around her died.

She'd seen one of the owners of the resort, Logan Graw, do the same, silence an entire room with his mere presence, except with him, everyone seemed intimidated.

Jordan wasn't intimidating. It hadn't taken her long to peg him as the social, outgoing type, always easy to smile. It was as if people gravitated toward him, quieting because everyone just acknowledged that he rightfully deserved to be the center of attention.

The staff called him Jordan, even if many in his position may have insisted on more formality to reinforce their status as manager. He didn't need to. Even with his affable manners, the man knew how to get things done his way. It was unnerving, the way he had people do exactly what he wanted without their even noticing that they were dancing like marionettes to his will. Lanie had the distinct feeling that she wouldn't be much different if she got too close to him.

Not that he was abusing his talent, or at least not as far as she knew, but Lanie was sure she couldn't risk being swept up in the fan club that included the female, and occasional male, staff members who were crushing on the manager.

As he took his position in front of everyone, wearing his usual khakis and polo shirt, she had to admit once again how good looking he was. It was really unfair for one man to have both his looks and charisma. If only he'd direct his charms elsewhere.

Like she always did when they were in a room together, Lanie stepped behind a group of maintenance guys and tried to fade into the background.

* * *

Jordan stepped into the noisy staff room down the hall from his office.

He'd carefully picked a time that would make it possible for everyone to be here, though some of the resort workers had to rush through their morning chores to make it on time. He'd have to look at the shift roster and allow those who had to work harder to be here some extra time off during the coming weekend.

Heads turned his way, and the animated chattering slowly faded.

"Hello, everyone," he started. "Thanks for coming together this morning. I have a couple of announcements to make."

Pausing briefly, he scanned the group, giving the people, most of whom he'd known his entire life, a smile. Like every day when his eyes started to wander around like this, he told himself he wasn't looking for her until, almost hidden in the back, he spotted her and an excited prickle ran through his body.

It was the same thing he'd been doing since she'd started working here. Whenever he knew she was around, he always looked for her.

Ever since she'd been in his office on the day of his best friend's wedding to apply for a job, she'd fascinated him. Most of the people working for him were locals like himself, people who had lived on this or other islands in the area their entire lives. It was rare to have newcomers and even rarer to have a beautiful woman who spoke several languages apply for work as a cleaner.

Maybe it was the fact that he'd been celebrating a wedding the day he'd met her, but he'd spent a few days wondering whether her appearance at the resort had been a sign from the universe. For years, he hadn't met a woman who caught his interest, and then suddenly, one showed up on the island out of nowhere. It was a ridiculous notion, of course. He hardly knew her, after all, but still, he seemed to look for her almost subconsciously whenever he walked around the resort.

Since he had no business stalking the poor woman, his infatuation was more of a curse than a blessing, especially since it went against his golden rule. Never sleep with resort guests or employees.

Still, besides his strange sentimentality that day, it was rare that people took him by surprise. Most people liked him, and he found it easy to get along with everyone, but Lanie gave him the impression that he had somehow bothered her from day one. Maybe that's why he had given her the job, because a strange voice in him wanted her to like him. Her reserve only made him more intrigued rather than feeling rejected.

Or, simply put, he was turning into a complete idiot.

He shook his head. Even if he felt more than ready to look for a woman to settle down with, there was no need to obsess over a woman who was obviously not interested.

Even so, he had to force his eyes away from her, training them instead on those standing in the front of the room.

"The first announcement is that we'll be getting some construction work done, so for a little while, I'll be working from my house, and the break room and storage room won't be accessible. The reception area won't be affected, so our guests won't notice much of the construction behind the scenes. But since you obviously need a space to take your breaks, we will use the main reception desk for marina business, and you're going to have the marina office as a break room while the workers finish up in here."

"What's being done?" a voice called.

"Some basic renovations mostly, but they'll also put in eco-friendlier air-conditioning units. Plus, and that is the second announcement I have, you'll get a proper changing room and showers."

Whoops and cheers sounded. Jordan knew how much the workers hated the lack of room to change out of their sweaty and sometimes dirty clothes after work. It had been a real oversight when the resort had been upgraded a few years back.

"There will be five showers, two for the women, two for the men, and one gender neutral one. The gender neutral one will have a small room attached to it for changing. Plus, there will be a changing room each for men and women with designated lockers for everyone."

When he left the room after answering some questions, Jordan was glad everyone seemed pleased. It hadn't been easy to convince Logan to create a budget for these renovations. Not that his friend didn't care for his employees, but he and his brothers had only inherited the resort from their father somewhat recently and had already poured quite a bit of money into expanding the eco-friendly luxury destination to attract a new clientele. Still, the Graw brothers had conceded when Jordan had made the case for the resort workers, as he knew they would.

Jordan crossed the hall into his office. He had to pack up everything he'd need in the coming weeks and move it to his house. Luckily, he lived in one of the villas on the island, so instead of trying to carve out a spot somewhere in the marina office where it would be crowded enough, he could just work from home.

Just as he sat down behind his desk, someone knocked on the door.

"Hey, Jordan," Gabriela said.

"Come in." He waved to the chair across from his desk. "What's up?"

"Great news about the showers. We sure need those. There are way too many sweaty men on the boat to Bocas." Gabriela waved her hand underneath her nose, grinning.

"Don't tell me women don't need to freshen up after a long day of work," he countered.

"You've got me there." She laughed.

"Actually, I'm here to talk to you about the party," Gabriela said, looking at him expectantly.

For a moment, Jordan felt taken aback. When Gabriela had first moved here to live with her aunt and work at the resort, she'd made it clear that she was interested in going out with him, but despite being much younger at the time, he'd quickly made sure she knew he didn't date employees of the resort. Or their family members, for that matter. She'd understood, and they'd moved on to an easy-going and friendly work friendship. Having her suggest that they do something outside of work was unusual.

"The party?" he asked carefully, knowing he was probably missing something obvious but was too distracted to put his finger on it.

Her laughter clued him in that he must be looking like a deer in the headlights, and he chuckled.

"Our midsummer party for the employees, dummy," Gabriela clarified. "It's in four weeks. Though you don't have to look quite so horrified by the suggestion of a party. You could use a night out and have some fun if you ever want to meet someone."

Before he could interject, Gabriela grinned. "Don't worry, I'm still well aware of your no-resort-employees rule, and I respect you more for it."

Rubbing his forehead, Jordan put on a crooked grin, downplaying his embarrassment. "The midsummer party, of course. I hadn't even considered it yet. Thanks for reminding me. I guess I'd better order everything for it soon."

"How about a party committee?" she suggested, eyes

sparkling with excitement.

"I suppose you have someone in mind?" Gabriela's excitement was palpable, and he didn't bother hiding his amusement.

"Well, if you ask so nicely, I'll be happy to organize things!" she responded with the expected enthusiasm.

"Thank you. That would be great. Let me know if you need anything from me."

"Anything?" she asked, waggling her eyebrows suggestively. This time, he didn't fall for her teasing.

"You're trouble, Gabriela, but whoever catches your attention will be a lucky guy."

"Nah, I'm good without a man in my life right now, thank you very much." With that, she left the office, leaving Jordan with the realization that he didn't feel the same way. He wanted someone in his life, and for that to happen, he needed to get himself a life outside of work.

He dismissed the image of Lanie wearing a pretty dress and dancing with him at the midsummer party. That wasn't going to happen.

CHAPTER 2

The marina office was much smaller than their usual break room. It wasn't intended for more than two or three people to work in, and Lanie had to squeeze her way to the back of the room, where she hoped she could put her bag for the day.

A hand closed around her arm, and for a second, she froze, looking for a possible escape route, before she recognized Alejandro, who often cleaned the pools of the villas she worked in.

"There is a small room around the corner that gets locked, if you want to put your purse there."

Lanie swallowed to get rid of her dry throat. "Uh, thanks."

Frustrated with herself, she walked around the corner to drop off her bag. Today was already off to a bad start, and it could only get worse. Avoiding Jordan completely had been an unreasonably optimistic goal from the start. He was her boss, after all, but that she'd been picked for the first cleaning rotation at his house while he worked there just seemed like a bad omen.

Since no amount of whining would help her, she picked up her supplies and started her round.

An hour later, and slightly worse for wear from the humidity, she was standing, cleaning caddy in hand, in front of his beautiful villa that looked as if it were designed for a millionaire, not a resort manager.

She would have tried to switch, but Gabriela hadn't been at work today, and since she kept to herself most of the time, she didn't exactly have much to go on with her coworkers. The last thing she needed was to draw attention to herself. She figured she'd just do her job and be in and out without having to talk to him. After all, he was working himself, so he wouldn't have time to chat with her.

Still, she fiddled with the hem of her uniform vest as she waited for him to open the door, unable to completely suppress the nervous energy.

"Come on in," a deep voice called from inside.

Coupled with his easygoing smile, Jordan's voice always seemed so light, it was like a melodic reflection of his open personality. Without seeing his face, though, his voice sounded a lot deeper, a lot more masculine, like a deep timbre that resonated in Lanie.

Stepping into the villa, she allowed herself a moment of curiosity.

A chest made of dark wood stood against the wall to her left. On her right, a staircase led upstairs. Straight ahead would be the living and kitchen areas. The layout was much the same as with the other private villas, since they had obviously all been built based on the same floorplan with only minor variations, but the decor in Jordan's place was unique.

As she made her way toward the main living space, Lanie noticed the wooden carvings that decorated the walls. There was a simple flower and a decal of a sailboat, but the most impressive piece was a scene of a woman standing at a beach. Fascinated, Lanie looked at it more closely.

She'd never seen something carved that expressed so much emotion. The face of the woman, even though it was small, seemed to radiate happiness. The waves behind her were equally small, but Lanie could almost hear the sound they would make as they shot forward to engulf the woman's feet in their white foam.

"That's my mother," a voice said from right behind her.

Lanie jumped and turned around. Retreating a step, her back bumped into the carving she had just admired. Her heart pounded, and she lifted a hand up to cover her mouth.

"I didn't mean to startle you," Jordan said with a slight chuckle, obviously amused by her reaction.

Lanie tried to calm her heart rate down enough to apologize when Jordan stepped forward, almost close enough for her breasts to touch his chest. For a moment, she had the crazy idea that he was about to kiss her, but then he merely reached out to hold on to the carving behind her.

"I'm rather fond of this one. I doubt I could recreate it, so I'd rather it stayed on the wall," he told her with a smirk.

"You made that?" Even to her own ears, her voice sounded incredulous.

"You didn't take me for an artist?" he asked, but his tone was teasing rather than insulted.

"I'm sorry, I didn't mean to break anything." Lanie took a step sideways and away from the wall. It felt oddly disappointing to bring back the distance between them, and she gave herself an internal scolding. She needed to stay far away from that man. It would do her no good to draw his attention.

"And you succeeded."

At Lanie's confused look, Jordan explained. "You didn't break the carving."

"Oh, right. Yes. Well, I'm glad." Trying to get back on track, Lanie looked around. "I'm here to do the cleaning. Where would you like me to start so I don't get in your way?"

There, that should ensure that she'd be able to keep away from him. Surely, he didn't want her to disrupt his work.

"You know what? I've set up my office in the living room while I'm working from home. You might as well start there and get that out of the way." Making his way toward the living area of the villa, he left her with no choice but to follow him.

"I don't actually have a home office. Usually, I prefer to leave my work where it belongs, but this seemed better than trying to squeeze into the marina office," Jordan explained as they entered the large space that combined the living and dining room with an open archway into the kitchen.

The oversized dining table held a laptop, an additional monitor, a printer, and several folders and notebooks. It looked like Jordan was one of those people who still worked with printed pages rather than having everything digital.

Lanie almost laughed at the irony that he was managing an eco-friendly resort.

"The marina office wouldn't even have enough space for one of these folders," she remarked, remembering the way the people from the morning shift had piled into the small office room this morning.

Jordan laughed. "Yeah, that's what I thought. I know it'll be tight for a couple of weeks, but at least it'll be really nice once the showers and changing rooms are ready."

"Yes, we appreciate the changes. Should I leave you to your work now?" Lanie hoped her voice sounded polite rather than desperate. The last thing she wanted to do was be rude to the man who'd given her a job when she hadn't been sure how she'd get through the coming weeks, but she really needed to get some distance between them.

Jordan gave her an intense look. Obviously, her attempt at being inconspicuous had failed. Under his stare, she could feel embarrassment color her cheeks.

"Yes, it seems we'd better get to work." He waved his hand in the general direction of a coffee maker. "Feel free to grab a cup of coffee whenever you'd like."

With that, he walked over to his desk, grabbing a mug of coffee from the kitchen island on his way. Ignoring the annoying voice inside her head that wanted to ask him what he was working on this morning, not even sure why she cared, Lanie scanned the room to determine what needed to be done.

This was what she did now, and it was honest work.

Forty minutes later, she'd straightened up both the downstairs and upstairs of the house, had cleaned the bathrooms, and had made sure the kitchen appliances were spotless. All that was left to do was a last sweep of the hallway floor, something she always left as her last task.

"All done?" Jordan asked from the opening of the hallway that led to the living space.

He'd been working the entire time, and they hadn't exchanged any words since she'd begun cleaning. If only he'd kept working for just a few minutes longer.

"Almost," she answered, hoping her curt reply would somehow discourage him from asking further questions.

No such luck.

"How are you liking the island so far? Is it very different from your previous home?"

Lanie almost sighed. She'd dreaded having this conversation with him. It was worse because he seemed so kind and interested, which only drove the point deeper that she'd become a liar. It didn't matter, though, because she had no room for mistakes.

Divert questions and lie if necessary. Besides 'stay as far away from Jordan Dane as possible', that had become another one of her mantras since moving here.

"I like it here. The work is good, and I found a nice place to live. I'm actually renting a room in a house that I share with two other women who work here."

"Mama Lita and Gabriela, right?"

Her head shot up to check his expression. He seemed unaware that it was strange that he already knew where she lived. Here she was, taking a risk by sharing details about her life that he didn't need to know, and he already knew them.

She'd promised herself not to turn paranoid once she left her home, but that was difficult when almost strangers knew where she lived before she ever mentioned anything about it. The resort was a relatively small place, and he was her boss with access to her file, sure, but it had enough workers that she didn't think he'd know exactly where everyone lived by heart, especially since she didn't live here on Howler Island but across the water in Bocas Town.

While her thoughts were racing, he had the nerve to chuckle. "Relax. Mama Lita brought you to your interview, remember? When I heard Gabriela say they had found someone to rent the extra room, I put two and two together."

"Oh, of course." Immediately, Lanie felt stupid for her overreaction. Way to give away her anxieties.

It was much too easy to forget that everyone here knew each other when she spent most of her time avoiding speaking with anyone despite the warm welcome she'd experienced. "I didn't mean to imply anything." She trailed off. She hadn't actually said anything wrong, so she shouldn't get defensive now.

"Don't worry," Jordan said before pausing. He gave her another inquisitive look. "You know, I'm actually a nice guy." His smile was brilliant, and Lanie understood all the young women, workers and guests alike, who got caught up in it. He was dangerously handsome, and it would do her no good to get distracted by that.

"Of course." To avoid having to hold his gaze, she bent down to grab her dustpan. Best that she didn't focus too much on his good looks and friendly attitude. "I'm very grateful you've given me this job, which I really should get back to now."

Jordan didn't immediately respond, and Lanie looked up to see why. He was looking at her with curiosity and something that looked like disappointment. Catching her looking, he shook his head slightly and gave her a small, resigned smile.

"Of course." He echoed her earlier words and turned to walk back to his make-shift office.

The feeling that she'd offended him irked her. Having a friendly boss should be something to be grateful for, and it stung that she'd become the type of person who shut down people who were only attempting to be nice to a newcomer. That wasn't her. At least it hadn't been her until she fled her home.

Just as Jordan stepped out of the hallway and into the living room, he turned back over his shoulder. "See you tomorrow morning!" His earlier smile was back in full force.

Excitement and dread flooded her simultaneously. For the rest of the week, she'd see Jordan Dane every morning.

* * *

Jordan let the folder he'd finished scanning fall onto the table.

It was annoying work to scan all the old files, and he really should have hired someone to do it, but he was particular in the way he liked to organize his files, and it was past due that all this old paperwork was digitized.

Bart Graw had been like a father to him, but despite his passion for self-sustainability and the environment, the old man hadn't taken to electronics. There hadn't even been internet on the island until Bart had died and his sons had taken over and renovated the resort.

Even though Jordan had known that these papers needed to be digitized for the past couple of years, he also knew that if he were being honest with himself, the woman whose presence seemed to rob him of all his concentration had been the main reason he'd spent the morning doing mindless scanning.

What was it about her?

Before his mother had gotten sick and told him the whole story about his father, there had been a time that he'd had the occasional fling with one of the female guests, but he'd never slept with an employee and would never do so in the future. He had better sense than that.

It wasn't like he wanted to spend his entire life alone, though. Recently, he'd been spending more time thinking about what he wanted for his future. Logan and Jane's wedding had only added fuel to those thoughts. Except it wasn't exactly easy to meet a woman if one worked as much as he did, and the women that he did see were either on the island for a brief vacation or they worked for him

He knew all too well that a relationship with someone who worked for him could be problematic, so why did the woman who was so clearly not interested in him make him question his careful rules? He really needed to get off the island more to improve his chances of meeting someone who was actually available.

The bars on the bigger island would be an option, but he wasn't in his twenties anymore and bars seemed like a terrible place to scout for a serious relationship. He could try online dating, but the thought alone made him want to roll his eyes. It was a cold day in hell that would happen.

That Bart's aversion to getting internet on the island had meant Jordan had also lived without it for many years probably had something to do with his current aversion to trying to make a meaningful connection with someone online. In more ways than one, Bart had an enormous influence on him, and the idea of his trying to date via messaging apps was about as likely to happen as Lanie suddenly developing an intense interest in spending time together.

Crossing the room, he opened the fridge and considered his options. Cold pasta salad, a sandwich, or some cereal. He checked the clock on the stove. It was eleven thirty. He grabbed the milk and poured himself a bowl of cornflakes. Looking at his food, he grinned. Maybe he wasn't grown up enough to find a woman to spend his life with just yet. Or maybe he needed to find a woman who enjoyed cooking. Wouldn't that be something?

When he finally closed his laptop that evening, Jordan wanted to groan. He enjoyed working in his office in the welcome center where there was always someone around for a quick chat. Here, there was nothing to pull him away from his work to take an occasional break, and his stiff shoulders told him he'd be better off bringing his comfortable office chair here for the next weeks if he didn't want to ruin his back.

Getting older sucked.

At least he had plans to see his friends this evening. Logan had invited him over for a barbecue, and Jordan welcomed the chance to catch up with him and Jane. In the past few weeks, he'd learned that Jane always had fun stories about her days with the mischievous monkey troops.

Since the two of them had only married recently, Jordan had wanted to give them time to themselves and hadn't visited as often as he would have otherwise liked. Still, it was great to have his best friend living back on the island after Logan had been gone building his eco-resort chain business for the past few years.

Jordan grabbed a bottle of wine that would go well with just about anything barbecued and walked toward his friends' place.

While he lived in one of the resort villas, Logan and Jane lived down a private lane that held a large house and three cottages that belonged to the three Graw brothers. Many of the workers called it Owner Road, and the name had caught hold, so even the Graws now used it.

Walking past the three cottages, Jordan made his way to the main house down the private lane, where a big kitchen and dining area had been used for family meals since the boys had been teenagers. When he knocked, Jane opened the door.

She was a good-looking woman. Her blonde hair usually hung in messy strands around her face, never quite staying in her ponytail or bun. Jordan had seen her with makeup only once, on her wedding day, but since then, he'd discovered that her face was more often streaked with dirt that matched the random leaves sticking out of her hair. Considering how Logan always managed to look as if he were ready to be photographed for *Forbes* magazine, the two made an interesting couple.

"Hey, Jordan, Logan is already out back." She greeted him with a smile, surprisingly without added dirt or leaves in her hair.

"Hey. I brought some wine for you." Handing over the bottle, he pulled Jane in for a quick hug.

His friend had chosen well, but Jordan didn't get to see Jane nearly enough since besides being a newlywed, she was also busy working on some new monograph that summarized her research findings about the female monkeys' howls, a project that she'd been busy studying when Logan had first met her. Still, she was now part of the Graw family and Jordan was intent on getting to know her even better. To him, she was family now.

"Jordan, get yourself out here," Logan called from the back where he stood next to the barbecue.

Walking over, Jordan let himself sink into the cushions of the two-seater that sat on the deck. From here he could see the ocean, a similar view to the one he had from his own back yard. It was a view that never got old.

He looked at his friend and saw the same content expression he was usually sporting these days. Yeah, it really looked like Logan had it all now.

Before he could go down the rabbit hole of self-pity, the smell of the barbecue drew his attention. "Man, I'm starving."

"Are you still living on pasta and sandwiches?" Logan laughed.

"Nah, I had something much more elaborate for lunch. Cereal!"

"You really need to grow up, man," Logan said, but he was grinning. "Seriously, though, try marriage. It's much better than that bachelor life, though it's usually safer when I do the cooking."

"We can't all capture a scientist in the wild," Jordan joked, though the raised eyebrow of his friend told him he hadn't been able to keep the note of melancholy out of his voice completely.

Grinning, he watched as Logan chuckled and flipped the burgers. Then his friend switched to a different tool and flipped the tofu skewers for his wife. Logan was all kinds of domesticated these days, thanks to Jane.

Soon, Jordan had ketchup dripping out of his mouth as Jane recounted an encounter she had with one of the island monkeys who'd stolen a protein bar from her.

"I was worried the Howler would eat the bar, which definitely isn't good for them, so I tried to convince her to bring it back in exchange for an apple. At first, I thought it worked well enough. She actually dropped the protein bar to get ahold of the apple, except then things went downhill because when I tried to pick up the bar, will you believe that she bombarded me with the apple?" Apparently, if the monkey wasn't allowed to have the protein bar, neither was Jane.

"How do you find working from home?" Logan asked Jordan when their plates were empty.

"It's not as easy to focus as it is in the office," Jordan said, his mind replaying images of Lanie.

"I prefer working in the Aualotta Relief compound, too. It makes it easy to separate work from home, and it helps me leave my work at the office at the end of the day."

Logan grinned. "Of course, she usually ends up getting distracted by her work anyway, and then I need to help get her focus back to our private life." The way he emphasized those last words made it very clear how he went about getting his wife's attention.

Jordan laughed as Jane blushed. "Good for you guys." He lifted his glass to them, and Jane actually giggled. It transformed her pretty but usually serious face into that of a blissfully happy woman.

Taking a drink of his wine, he leaned back into the pillows of the deck chair to relax his back.

"Speaking of your home, Jordan," Jane said, "how come you decided to buy one of the villas and don't have a cottage here with the rest of the Graw men?"

The easy way Jane lumped him in with her husband and brothers-in-law was nice, and her question was one he'd asked himself before. Until four years ago, he'd lived in the old cottage his mother had rented from Bart Graw when she'd still been alive. It had been easy to simply stay there, and he didn't consider himself someone who needed a fancy house to be happy.

Usually, he only lived on his manager's salary, which wouldn't have been enough to pay for building a brand-new house anyway, even a relatively small cottage, but when he'd learned of the renovation plans and the villas that Logan and Ben had settled on, he'd made an exception.

"I had some money saved, and I guess it was time for me to actually get a place of my own. I figured that with the villas already being planned, it was the easiest to just get in on the plan."

"Actually," Logan jumped in, "what Jordan isn't saying is that he had more money than he knew what to do with because he made a very smart investment in a certain very savvy businessman."

Logan had been thrilled when Jordan had told him he wanted to build one of the villas for himself, pleased that Jordan had finally given him an opportunity to do something for the trust Jordan had placed in him when he was just a young man starting out. What Logan had never understood was that the money that had meant so much to him back then had meant nothing to Jordan.

Ignoring Logan's pleased-with-himself grin, Jordan turned to Jane. "Were you always attracted to arrogant men, or did this one just hide his real nature until now?" He motioned toward Logan, and Jane laughed.

"No, I pegged him for what he is pretty quickly."

"And you love me for it!" Logan stated confidently. "It's true, though. Jordan invested heavily in Graw Resorts when I was just getting started, and I couldn't have done it without his help, so it's only fitting that he now owns one of the villas here."

What Logan left out was that without the money his mother had left him, Jordan wouldn't have been able to invest in Logan's business to begin with. Being raised by a hard-working single mother, no one around assumed that he'd inherited much. His mom had been wonderful and had worked hard to give them a good life. When she'd gotten sick and the chemo hadn't done what it should, leaving her with a tumor in her lungs, she'd told him about the money he would inherit, courtesy of his biological father, a rich guy who'd taken off on her at the end of his stay on Howler Island.

Jordan hadn't known the man had sent his mother money each year that she'd put away for him, and he certainly hadn't wanted anything to do with the money at the time. Instead, he'd invested it in his friends' businesses when they needed help getting started. Logan's eco-resort chain had turned into a million-dollar company, and Ben's construction business had grown with it since Graw Construction handled the building of the resorts. With his friends' successes, Jordan had become wealthy, but he'd still refused to touch the money until after Bart's death.

"So, were you involved in the redesign of the resort?" Jane asked.

"Sure, I dealt with all the coordination between Graw resorts and Graw construction. It was simpler to have someone who was actually on the island organizing things." Jordan would have to ask Logan whether he'd told Jane about his share in the company at some point. Not that he cared either way, since Jane was part of the Graw family now.

Even today, he worked happily as an employee of the resort even though he was a silent shareholder, something that would have shocked all the resort workers who worked with him on a daily basis.

Logan nodded. "Yeah, neither Ben nor I wanted to come here much after Dad passed. It was good to have Jordan onsite. And of course, he helped us choose which villas to go with. Ben had pre-selected a few designs, and then Jordan picked out the one he liked best for himself. We ended up just going with that design for the rest of the villas."

"That's true. If I'd left it up to them," Jordan said, "they would've probably just picked one at random."

"True enough," Logan agreed. "They were all eco-friendly designs, so I was happy, and Ben had already narrowed it down for us. Jake doesn't really care about style, so Jordan was the one who still had a stake in making the decision. You know, after he finally decided to go for it and built a place for himself."

Logan wasn't wrong about Jordan having taken a long time to make the decision to move out of the old cottage that had belonged to his mom. It had taken him years to touch the money his father had sent. It was only when Bart had passed away a few years ago, surprising Jordan by including him to a small degree in his will alongside his sons, that Jordan had decided to dip into the money he'd invested in his friends' successes.

Bart's last testament had reaffirmed that Howler Island would always be Jordan's home, and when the Graw brothers had decided on building the new eco-friendly villas, he'd finally decided that the money didn't tie him to his biological father. What he did with that money would decide who he was, and by building a house for himself on Howler Island, he'd claimed his home.

He'd used the money as a building block for his future. Howler Island was where his mother had raised him and where Bart Graw had included him in his family alongside the Graw brothers, and he now had a home where he'd one day raise his own children.

But first, he'd have to find a woman who shared the same dream.

CHAPTER 3

After a heavy rainfall in the early morning, the sun was already burning down, and the seat of the golf cart was burning through Lanie's uniform as she drove to Jordan's villa for the second day of her cleaning rotation there. Like most mornings, she'd dropped off her bag and gone straight to work, too distracted to make conversation and watch her every word. She needed to consider her options.

She wouldn't be able to avoid Jordan for the rest of the week since she still had another four days during which she'd have to clean his house while he was working in his makeshift home office. This meant that she could either avoid him as best as possible and try to keep their interactions as brief as possible or she could just suck it up and engage with him when he didn't give her any other choice. If she made sure he liked her well enough, she might just fade in with all the other workers he spoke with on a daily basis. Of course, she'd need to do that without revealing too much about herself at the same time.

Since the first option, avoidance, hadn't done much to discourage him yesterday, it seemed that today she'd have to attempt option two. Most people were happy to talk about themselves when given the opportunity, so she'd simply have to give him enough opportunities for that to prevent him from asking her too many questions in return.

Otherwise, her usual mantra would have to suffice. Divert questions, lie if necessary.

"Come in," Jordan's voice called when she knocked, and she stepped into the air-conditioned entryway.

Staying far away from any of the carvings on the walls, Lanie placed her supplies to the side and went back out to grab the vacuum. Once she'd collected that, she leaned over the cleaning caddy and grabbed a pair of washable shoe covers. The resort didn't like to use the disposable kind since the whole point was to keep things eco-friendly.

As she pulled the covers over her shoes to make sure she didn't leave the place messier than it was before she came, she could hear footsteps behind her.

Why couldn't the man just focus on his work and leave her to do hers?

"Excuse me," a pleasant baritone voice said from behind her. Not Jordan's voice.

"Oh." Lanie jumped a bit. "I'm sorry. I didn't mean to be in the way."

"Not at all," the man answered, and when she turned around, Lanie realized he was no other than Logan Graw, owner of the entire resort.

"Mr. Graw. I'm sorry."

Friendly lines appeared in the usually serious looking face. Not that she'd spoken with him this closely before.

"What are you sorry for? It looks to me like you're busy doing your job, which I appreciate."

Lanie was still staring at Logan Graw when Jordan appeared in the hallway behind him. "Are you terrorizing my staff?" he asked, humor lacing his voice.

"Your staff?" Logan retorted, clearly amused.

"Yeah, you're just corporate, didn't you know that?"

Jordan was so obviously confident in his place here on the island that he didn't mind joking with his boss. If only she could say the same.

The way he grinned could only be described as roguish, and she found her eyes glued to him. Jordan was everything she found attractive in a man. He was friendly, funny, approachable, and kind. He also had all the things she wanted, a stable and rewarding job, friends, and most importantly, a place to call home.

And he's off limits, she reminded herself quickly.

"Well, that explains why I need to go home and get on my conference call about the new bird sanctuary," Logan said, startling Lanie out of her reverie.

She quickly grabbed hold of the caddy and started up the stairs before Logan left and Jordan could try to start a conversation. Unfortunately, when she'd just reached the upstairs and heard the door close behind the resort owner, footsteps on the stairs told her she hadn't escaped Jordan just yet.

Trying to ignore the strange feelings of nerves and anticipation, she moved through the bedroom and further to the en suite bathroom. Behind her, she could hear Jordan come into the bedroom. Ignoring him, she donned the rubber gloves that, after a long day of wearing them, made her hands feel as if she'd been in the bathtub a little too long. Then she started running water to scrub the already clean countertops.

By the time she finished the counters and the rest of the bathroom, she'd decided that Jordan must have just grabbed something from his room and gone back downstairs, but when she stepped into the bedroom, he was lying on the bed, his hands propped behind his head, eyes closed.

He looked incredible. His hair was tousled in a way that made it look as if a woman had run her hands through it. His jeans rode low enough that the top of his underwear was showing, and his button-up shirt made it look like he'd been at work when someone had teased him away from important business to roll in the sheets.

The image was so vivid and the thought so unexpectedly arousing that she felt heat rush to her cheeks. It was much too strange to walk in on him like this.

Should she try to just walk past him as silently as she could? Or should she say something? And why had he followed her just to lie here on his bed in the first place?

Before she could make up her mind, his eyes opened.

"Hello, Lanie." He smiled. "I didn't get the chance to actually greet you earlier."

"Did you wait here the whole time just to say hello?" Her voice sounded almost accusing, and she cringed internally. Way to be likable and not stand out.

He laughed, the sound allowing her to relax a little. "No, of course not. I would've come into the bathroom to say hey, but I didn't want to startle you again. You looked a bit unnerved earlier. I really just came up to grab a book I was reading last night and decided to close my eyes for a moment. I've got a bit of a headache."

"Oh, I'm sorry," Lanie said, realizing she was repeating the phrase a lot today. What was wrong with her that she acted like a socially inept weirdo? She needed to get her paranoia under control. That had been the entire point of leaving her home and coming here, to start over somewhere where she didn't need to be so tense all the time.

"Don't be. It's not all that bad."

Shoulders sagging, she returned his smile. He really was being nice, and she needed to get herself in check. "That's good."

Even though she was trying to be less weird, it still felt awkward being in his room while he was lying on his bed. Why did he have to look so good? Wasn't it enough that he had this magnetic personality everyone seemed to adore? She lowered her eyes, not wanting to keep looking at him as he was relaxing in his own bedroom.

There was no way she wanted him to sense that she was attracted to him. That wouldn't help her stay unnoticed. Maybe she should just walk out? Would that be rude or the professional thing to do? She didn't want him to think she was acting suspiciously.

Before she'd decided, he spoke again. "I should get

back to work, anyway."

Looking up, she watched as he got up from the bed in a fluid motion, leaving him standing between her and the door to the hallway. Her eyes flitted between him and the door, expecting him to walk out and release her from this awkward situation.

He obviously noticed her look and eagerness to get out of his bedroom, and his face turned into a strangely impassive mask. With a few quick steps, he left the room, only to turn back around once he was in the hallway. "I should be the one apologizing. I didn't mean to get in your way while you do your job." His voice sounded formal and without his usual warmth.

When he walked away, guilt for making this usually so happy and sociable guy retreat coursed through her.

The rest of the day, Jordan kept his distance, and when Lanie arrived at his house the next morning, she felt strangely subdued. This was what she'd wanted, for him to just let her do her job, so why was it so disappointing that he didn't come to the door or even call out a hello?

Should she go to him and say hi? She could just walk down the hallway, peak her head into the living area where he worked, and quickly say good morning. Then she could disappear upstairs and keep her distance again. That would be the polite thing to do, wouldn't it?

Before she could overthink it, she started down the hallway and took one step into the living area only to find that Jordan wasn't sitting at his desk. He also wasn't in the kitchen, and she turned around, feeling a little disappointed. She could see that the bathroom door in the hallway stood slightly ajar, and he wasn't in there either.

Maybe he was upstairs?

The thought that he may be lying in his bed again, eyes closed and his boxer shorts peaking out at his waist, made a warmth spread through her body.

With more enthusiasm than was a good idea, she leaned down to grab her cleaning caddy and started up the stairs. Anticipation coiled inside her as she kept her steps light, walking toward his bedroom.

She should have stayed downstairs, of course, and cleaned there while he was gone. It would have been the smart thing to do. Maybe he was sick and needed to rest. He'd had a headache yesterday, and it could have gotten worse. She shouldn't sneak up on him like this. It was wrong, for him and for her. And still, her feet carried her closer to the bedroom door.

This door, too, stood slightly ajar, and she gently nudged it open.

Inside, the room was empty. So was the bathroom.

Lanie sat down on the bathtub for a moment, chiding herself for her own idiocy. This was good. This was for the best.

* * *

Standing with Logan, Jordan watched the contractors lean over the schematics and point out why they wanted to move one of the walls a bit further in. He didn't need to be here, but he hadn't wanted to stay in his house when Lanie arrived.

The way she'd looked yesterday, as if she were a trapped animal that felt threatened by him, wouldn't leave him alone. He could see in hindsight how his behavior may have been misunderstood as inappropriate. He'd lain down on his bed, feeling exhausted from a late night of reading through a marketing book that Logan had recommended to him, and his head had hurt.

The fact that she'd thought he'd waited there for her to come out of the bathroom and the way her eyes had flitted to the door when he'd stood up, almost as if she were worried he was trying to cut off her exit, had made him feel like some pervert who'd tried to intimidate his employee.

The exact thing he did everything to avoid. He'd never abuse his power or intentionally intimidate a woman—or a man, for that matter.

And yet, Lanie had clearly been uncomfortable in his presence. Maybe she'd had some bad experience in the past with an employer and that's why she'd come without references. It would explain her hesitance in all their interactions.

As much as he didn't want to think she'd ever suffered sexual harassment, the idea that it wasn't specifically him she felt uncomfortable about was strangely reassuring. Her jumpiness around Logan yesterday helped to confirm that suspicion.

So, here he was, avoiding his house. Avoiding Lanie. And still, she was consuming his thoughts. He just didn't get why. She was beautiful, yes. But more than her looks, it was his protective instinct that drew him closer to her. Parts of him wanted to reassure and protect her from the very threat she seemed to sense in him.

But at the same time, he couldn't deny that her curves were the perfect shape for him to run his hands over. Her dark hair fell in strands that would look perfect flung over a pillow, and her eyes were huge and could trap a man. But she was also standoffish, so he really had no right to even think of her in that way. Not that she was rude, per se. She just seemed uncomfortable around him.

So why did he want to spend time with her when he hardly even knew the woman?

He needed to give her the room she wanted, which was partly why he wasn't at his house now. He was trying to be a gentleman. At least, that sounded a lot better than being a coward who didn't trust himself not to lust after a woman who clearly wasn't interested.

When the contractor suddenly walked out of the room, Jordan realized he'd completely zoned out of the meeting.

"What's up with you today?" Logan asked, eyebrows raised.

"I think I need to get laid."

Logan's surprised sputter of laughter was followed by an inquisitive stare. "Really? That doesn't seem like your usual M.O." His friend let the statement hang between them, and Jordan scrambled to figure out how to reply to that.

It really wasn't his usual style. He didn't like the idea of one-night stands. Not that he hadn't tried a couple of times, but it just wasn't what he was looking for, especially in the past few years. It had been a big part of the reason he'd needed to leave the island for a few months before being back now to do his job again.

Sometime last year, or maybe even a little before then, Jordan had started to find it difficult to figure out what he wanted out of his life when he was still living in the exact place he'd grown up. Nothing about his life had changed except that the resort he now managed was much more profitable and attracted richer clientele. His life had become monotonous despite the job that he loved doing.

All four Graw brothers who'd grown up with him on Howler Island had moved on, created their own lives for themselves elsewhere. Many of the people who stuck around here did so because their economic status didn't permit many other options. Of course, there were also those people who simply wanted to stay. After all, it was a beautiful place to live, and Jordan had always figured he was one of them.

He'd never had the desire to leave, even though he had the money to do so. At least, that had been true until last year when he'd started to doubt whether he'd ever find the things he wanted here.

He had no idea what had triggered it, but the feeling had grown stronger and stronger until one day, he'd simply booked a plane ticket and called Logan to tell him he needed a leave of absence for a few months.

Then, while he was gone, he'd finally come to a realization. Howler Island was the right place for him. It didn't matter that he hadn't gone somewhere else to grow into his own life. He'd simply been lucky to be born where he was happy to live. But traveling had driven home the point that he didn't want to be alone anymore.

A one-night stand wouldn't fix that problem.

"Yeah, you're right. But I've got to get my head on straight."

Clearly intrigued now, Logan sat down on Jordan's office desk. It was currently covered in a plastic tarp to protect it from the construction debris, but Logan didn't seem to care despite his fancy dress pants. Jordan himself preferred to wear thin linen pants at work since he wasn't in the mood for sweating his balls off every day. Luckily, the dress code was relaxed as long as he didn't have meetings scheduled.

"What's going on?"

Logan wasn't the type to pry, but he was Jordan's closest friend and obviously wanted to give him the opportunity to talk if he needed to. Unfortunately, admitting to another owner of the resort that he had the hots for an employee seemed like an HR nightmare. Not that he'd done anything inappropriate.

At least, not on purpose.

Still, he didn't mind sharing some of what was bothering him. Logan knew him well enough that he'd understand how Jordan felt.

"Do you want to get some beers over in Bocas on Friday?" he asked, avoiding a direct answer. It would be good to have a night out, and perhaps he could get a feel for what the dating scene was like at the same time. Finding his future wife in a bar seemed unlikely, but at this point, he might as well keep an open mind.

"Sounds good. It's been ages since we did that."

Maybe Logan could help him figure out how to avoid succumbing to online dating and lusting after a woman he had no right to pursue. A woman who may or may not still be in his house when he returned home in a minute.

The thought stayed with him the entire walk to his house.

As he stepped inside, he heard humming from the main living area. So, she was still here. Jordan wasn't sure why that made him feel relieved when he'd just spent the morning essentially hiding from her after yesterday's fiasco.

Deciding he should just act like he would with any other of the cleaners, he strode through the living room toward the kitchen area, making sure to keep his expression neutral and only giving her a small smile that wouldn't look as if he were trying to flirt.

"Hello, Lanie."

This time, she'd clearly heard him come in because she was already turned toward the hallway when he entered.

"Good morning," she said, her voice sounding strangely cheerful. Except, when she scanned his face, her brows knitted together in a confused look. Before he could ask her what was wrong, she quickly recovered and plastered her bright smile back on. There was a good chance his own smiling face looked similarly forced.

Well, at least he'd been right about yesterday having been awkward for them both. This was ridiculous. They were adults, and it was obvious that they needed to clear the air or this would just get more and more strange, and if anyone noticed this tension between them, he could only guess how the rumors would start flying. There was nothing like a small island to make sure everyone was up in everyone else's business.

He might as well get it over with. The idea that she considered him a threat didn't sit right with him, anyway.

Stepping back to the kitchen island so that she'd know he was giving her space, he made eye contact. "Lanie, I wanted to apologize if my behavior yesterday seemed out of line in any way. I really didn't mean for you to feel uncomfortable in my presence, and I want you to know that I will certainly keep my distance."

Watching her expression carefully, he tried to determine what she was thinking, but she just continued to look at him as if her expression were frozen in place.

After a moment, she sucked her lower lip into her mouth as if to chew on it, and he shifted his weight uncomfortably. You wouldn't think that with his nervous tension, there would be even the slightest glimmer of a chance that he'd get aroused, and yet here he was, even though it was the last thing he should be feeling right now.

Annoyed with himself, he quickly turned away from Lanie, no longer wanting to watch her. Striding around the kitchen island, he went to work on brewing himself a coffee. He wasn't even sure he wanted to drink it, but he needed something to do, and he doubted that sitting himself down in front of the computer would be enough of a distraction. He needed to keep his hands busy without needing to think because thinking was clearly going poorly at the moment.

"Thank you, and I'm sorry," her voice sounded from behind him. She'd spoken softly, almost too quiet, but he'd been so focused on her that he heard the quaver in her voice.

He turned back around, needing to read her body language and make sure he didn't misunderstand anything she said.

"Why are you sorry?"

For a moment, he thought she wouldn't answer, but then she pulled her shoulders back and looked directly at him. It was only now that he noticed how rarely she did that. She'd avoided him even in this small way, never looking him directly in the eyes if she had a choice, and he couldn't help but be startled by the confident expression she wore now.

This woman was different from anyone he'd met before. An enigma of sorts.

A beautiful enigma.

"I'm apologizing because even though you gave me this job and you've been kind and welcoming to me, I haven't made more of an effort to return your kindness. My behavior was rude. Please accept my apology."

Her eyes looked at him with such earnestness, something akin to desperation, that Jordan got the feeling that she was trying to ask for forgiveness for more than her standoffish behavior. Though he couldn't guess at what she meant, there was no way he could deny her.

"Apology gladly accepted. Now, how about we start

over?"

It took her a moment to respond again, as if every response she gave him had to be weighed carefully in her mind. Had he seemed overeager again? This woman made him keep questioning his own behavior.

Finally, she spoke again. "Yes, let's." Then she gave him a smile.

It was the first time since he'd given her the job that she looked at him with an honest and open smile, and she'd never looked as beautiful as now.

For some reason, this small smile felt more like a win than anything he'd accomplished in a long while.

CHAPTER 4

On Thursday, Lanie didn't feel the same hesitation when she entered Jordan's villa.

His willingness to put himself out there and apologize for the strange moment in his bedroom had reminded her that they were adults and that not every man was going to turn her life into hell. As often as she told herself not to give in to paranoia, his open apology had been a lot more successful in giving a her a much-needed reality check.

Life was moving on, and she should too.

She still wasn't entirely sure why he'd apologized when she'd been the one acting weird, but she appreciated his effort to make her comfortable. The least she'd been able to do was to put on her big girl panties and behave like the polite person she wanted to be.

Though she probably shouldn't use panty analogies.

Definitely no thinking about panties, or underwear, or anything down there when around her boss.

With more enthusiasm than she'd felt since she'd started this job a month ago, she walked up to the living area, cleaning caddy in hand. She would no longer actively try to avoid Jordan. Instead, she'd say hello and clean the room he was in first. It would be her way to show him he didn't make her feel uncomfortable. Well, not for the reasons he may think, anyway.

She was still uneasy about the possibility that he'd ask her too many questions about herself, of course, but she could never truly start a new life here if she didn't at least attempt to let go of those fears and actually start making friends.

"Good morning," she said as she entered the room.

Jordan was sitting behind his desk. He'd apparently gotten a proper office chair to sit in, and the table was free of the scattered piles of paper that had been there before. Instead, he was working only on a laptop, a single coffee mug sitting on the table next to him.

His smile rewarded her for coming in here first. There was no question about it. It was this smile that made people like him. Wide, open, and friendly. He didn't hold anything back and seemed genuinely pleased to be around people.

Mama Lita had welcomed her with such kindness, Gabriela had accepted her as their new roommate with friendliness, and Jordan was showing her nothing but genuine pleasure at having her around. At least when she wasn't acting strangely. And still, she'd been holding on to her fear that she'd have to leave again. It was time to let go of that.

"Good morning," Jordan said with his cheerful voice.

"I thought I'd start in here today, if that's all right with you?"

"By all means," he said and looked pleased. It was as if she were doing him a favor.

Turning around to get started, Lanie could feel her own smile. Somehow, she could feel optimistic again, and it was such a relief that in the following thirty minutes, her smile didn't fade once.

This island could very well be her new forever home, however much that made her sound like an animal rescued from a shelter. She'd rescued herself, and now it was her job not to stay in her own way of finding happiness here. She deserved to have a second chance at a good life.

It was only when the clatter of Jordan's typing seized that she realized she'd been humming to herself.

She looked up at him, knowing her cheeks were

flushed with embarrassment. Now she'd gone and interrupted his work. But once again, Jordan seemed perfectly happy, not in the least irritated by her humming.

"What song was that? I like the melody."

"I'm not sure, actually. It's one my mum always used to sing. I never heard the original, I think. But I always liked listening to it."

"My mum used to sing around the house too, but usually something that she got stuck in her head because it was playing on the radio. She worked here as a cleaner too, actually."

Lanie took a step toward Jordan, surprised and intrigued. "Your mom was a cleaner at this resort?"

"Yes. Well, technically, it wasn't a resort then. It was only a hotel before the Graw brothers inherited it. She worked for their father, Bart Graw."

"So, you grew up here? Does she still live on the island then?" Lanie asked before thinking better of it. It'd been a while since she'd allowed herself to ask people questions about themselves unless it had been a means to distract them from her. She didn't want people to reciprocate with questions of their own, but she couldn't help her curiosity.

She hadn't expected that Jordan's mother had worked as a cleaner here herself. It explained his kindness toward all the resort workers, and she wondered how many of the older people on the island had already known him when he'd been a little boy.

"My mum passed away eight years ago, but yes, I grew up here. I recently traveled a bit, and I still think it's the most beautiful place in the world to call home."

Behind Jordan, the windows allowed her to look out toward the ocean and a smaller, uninhabited island was visible in the distance. Even from here, she could see that despite the season, the sun was sparkling on the water.

It was a beautiful place to live.

When she'd chosen her flight to come here, she hadn't planned her destination, simply taking the next best connecting flights she was able to afford, but she couldn't deny that if she'd been in the right state of mind to choose a place to start over, this would have sounded perfect.

She gave Jordan a smile because he'd once again reminded her that she was here to live her life, not just to hide. Howler Island was her home now, too. "It really is beautiful."

"So, what made you move here?" he asked, and immediately, Lanie stepped back from him. It was an instinctive action, not calculated, but she could see his brows furrow.

"I'm sorry. I didn't mean to be nosy."

Shaking her head, she forced herself not to overreact at the simple question, though clearly, it was already a little late for that. "No, no, you're not being nosy. It really was a stroke of luck. But I'd love to know about the history of this place. You said it only turned into a resort recently?"

After a moment, Jordan nodded, apparently accepting her change of topic. "How about this? I'll grab us each a glass of orange juice and then I'll tell you a bit about the island."

"I should work," Lanie tried to argue, but he'd already gotten up, shaking his head in amusement. "I know for a fact that you're allowed to take a morning break, and I promise we'll both get back to work once we finish our drinks."

She could feel herself nod. Something about this man was just too magnetic to resist. Lanie watched as he went to the kitchen cabinet and pulled out two glasses, filled them with juice, and then turned back to her.

"Come on, we'll sit on the balcony. Might as well get some fresh air while we're at it."

When they stepped outside, the humidity washed over her, no doubt making sure her baby hairs were curling around her face in the wild way that no hair product could tame. Not that she was wasting money on hair products these days, anyway.

Before sitting down on the cream-colored cushions of the deck chair, Lanie looked down at her uniform. She hadn't done any cleaning that left her with dust all over, and he'd been the one to suggest sitting out here, so she figured she was okay.

Sitting down, she looked up to find Jordan watching her with that focused expression he sometimes got when he didn't realize she'd caught him looking at her. Not wanting to give him the opportunity to take this conversation somewhere unexpected, she quickly followed up on her earlier question. "So, how did you become a resort manager? Your mom must have been especially proud since she also worked here."

His eyes crinkled as if her question made him happy. "Well, you've met Logan. His father, Bart, came to the island when it was still relatively cheap to buy the land. When he met his wife, Selina, they decided to build and run a small hotel. They hired my mum, and she lived on the island in a small apartment that was part of the hotel.

"My mum and Selina ended up falling pregnant with Logan and me at the same time, even though Logan's parents were quite a bit older than my mum. She was only eighteen then. Anyway, Logan and I inevitably became best friends. Logan's two younger brothers too, really, since there were no other kids around this side of the island. Unfortunately, Bart's wife passed away while giving birth to the youngest one, Ben, when Logan was only five.

Anyway, the Graw brothers all moved away after we graduated high school, but I decided to do long-distance studies to get my business degree so I stayed. Bart Graw hired me, and I helped him run the place as he got older. When he passed away, Logan and his brothers inherited the hotel and turned it into the resort it is today. He left me a smaller percentage too, and I stayed on to run the place."

As Jordan paused his story, Lanie noticed she hadn't even taken a sip from her orange juice. Quickly, she lifted the glass to her lips and drank some, trying to decide whether to ask the question she was most curious about.

"You look like you want to ask something," Jordan said, reading her too well.

"Well, I do, but I'm afraid it would be a rude question."

"You want to know about my father," he guessed, and Lanie nodded, grateful she hadn't been the one to say it. Apparently, Jordan had expected it, though.

"Most everyone around here knows, anyway. It's too small a place for gossip not to make the rounds, even so many decades after the fact," he said.

Leaning forward, he put his own glass of juice on the small table. It was still full, too. "My mum had just started working at the hotel when a man rented out a room for two months. Apparently, he was there to plan for an important project at work. He was wealthy, so he could afford to take two months away from his company to focus on a special project, but he also sought anonymity, which is why he chose this small island with a family-run hotel. To make the story short, my mother fell madly in love with him and ended up pregnant. He left the island soon after, never to be seen again."

A muscle in Jordan's cheek was twitching slightly, and for a moment he lost the warm and inviting aura he usually wore. Lanie immediately regretted having encouraged him to tell the story. Obviously, he still resented his father for leaving.

"I'm sorry," she told him, unsure what else she could say.

"Don't be. She truly loved him, you know? She told me that when she got sick. She said she never regretted those two months with him, not just because she had me, but because she'd had the chance to find out what falling in love feels like." Shaking his head, Jordan looked at the ocean for

81

a moment and then picked up his glass again, drinking a big gulp.

"I don't understand why people let others get away with treating them so poorly and end up calling it love, especially when others get hurt in the process." Her words stumbled out before she could hold them back. Hopefully, Jordan would only relate them to his own situation. Still, her words revealed more than she'd intended to, and she raised her own glass to her lips, letting the fresh flavor of citrus wash away the taste of bitterness that coated her tongue.

Why did people seem to turn blind toward a person when they thought they were in love?

Jordan only looked at her, the emotions in his eyes hard to read, and for a moment they both sat there, not saying anything.

"I still believe in love." His words hung between them until his expression turned back into his usual smile, and Lanie couldn't help but feel herself even more drawn to him at his declaration.

"Even though your own father left your mother?"

"Yes, despite that," he said with conviction in his voice. Then he asked, "Have you met Jane yet?"

It took Lanie a moment to realize whom he was speaking about.

"Logan Graw's wife? I haven't exactly met her, but I know who she is." They'd been waving at each other for several weeks now, and Lanie had heard she was incredibly smart and committed to her work.

"Exactly, her. She came to the island for a few months to do research here. Then she met Logan, fell in love, and bam, they both decided to move here full-time. So yes, I believe in love. But don't get me wrong, as much as I'm a sucker for a romantic twist, I won't repeat my mother's mistake. I know better than to hope that a brief fling will be enough to convince someone to give up their entire life and move to the island. That stuff doesn't normally happen, even if Logan and Jane got lucky. Still, that doesn't mean I can't hold out for a woman who will be happy to share her life with me."

* * *

Drinking his juice, Jordan tried to hide the confusion he felt as he watched Lanie. For the life of him, he couldn't quite figure out why he'd told her about his father. Or why he'd mentioned that Bart had included him in his will.

After Bart's passing, when he'd learned about his inheritance, he'd been surprised, but none of the Graw brothers had questioned why Jordan had also inherited from their father. Logan, his best friend, had been pleased, but it had been Jake who'd really surprised Jordan when he'd told him, *of course you got part of the place, brother, you've always held it together for us. Without you, the place wouldn't have run all these years.*

Still, he hadn't wanted the workers to know about his having been included in Bart's will. It wasn't because he wanted to make a secret out of the wealth gap between him and many of his employees but because this place had never felt like a business, more like his family. At the time, he'd been worried that if he were no longer viewed as just another employee, even if one in a higher position, then it might change the dynamic he had with the people on the island.

Maybe it had been a ridiculous decision, but now, four years after Bart's death, it seemed strange to suddenly announce it to everyone. It would seem as if he'd lied rather than simply not shared the information.

And yet, he'd just told Lanie and he couldn't figure out why.

Fortunately, Lanie was too caught up in the drama of his father's defection to follow up on his other revelation. Since she was new here, she probably didn't think anything of it.

Unfortunately, his assumption only held true until her next question.

"So let me get this straight. You grew up here when the place was still a small, family-run hotel. Your mom and the older Mr. Graw were both single parents, and then when the owner passed away, you actually inherited part of the place?" She raised her eyebrows, implying the obvious question instead of asking it out right.

"You think my mom and Bart may have been more than employer and employee?"

"Well, I don't know. I mean, if you knew him for your entire life and you worked for him, supporting him when his own sons had left the island, I suppose he would've had enough reason to include you in his will as it is, but the thought crossed my mind. I mean, they were on this secluded, beautiful island together, and I imagine raising boys by themselves was challenging. It doesn't seem absurd that they may have leaned on each other and become more than friends after a while."

She was perceptive. He and Logan had wondered the same thing once they'd been older, though neither of them had ever ended up asking Bart about it. They knew Bart had loved his wife Selina and had missed her. Pictures of her had been placed all over his house, but it was certainly possible that he and Jordan's mom had been more than friends.

"I honestly don't know, but I hope for her sake that they did. That the only love she found abandoned her isn't exactly the thing you wish for anyone. She never dated to my knowledge, or at least she kept it a secret from me. With my being a self-involved teenage boy who had his hang-ups about the way my father knocked up my mom, she probably didn't want to put any more on my plate by introducing me to any men she may have been seeing. And then she passed away at forty. I was only twenty-one when she died. Pretty young, all things considered. And after she'd passed, I never asked Bart. She got cancer, and it wasn't an easy way for her to die. I think once she was gone, I needed time to breathe for a while."

Sipping her orange juice, Lanie watched him, and again, he wondered why he was telling her all this. Something about the way she listened drew him in, or maybe he just kept talking to spend more time with her, his strange fascination with this woman dictating his behavior.

"In that case, I hope that whatever connection your mom and Bart had brought them some measure of happiness," she said, and her words reflected the woman she must be behind her reserved façade. Someone kind who wanted people to have a good life despite the obstacles they faced.

"What about your parents?" he asked, curious about the people who'd raised a woman who earnestly cared for others' happiness and equally intrigued to finally find out a little more about Lanie. He knew almost everything about the people who worked here, knew their families and life stories, but he knew next to nothing about Lanie, and something told him there was a lot to learn.

She smiled, her face getting a distracted look as she answered. "They are still happily married. Honestly, if such a thing as soul mates exists, then my parents are that."

Interesting. Given her earlier comment about people using love as an excuse for mistreating others, it'd made him wonder if she was a skeptic when it came to relationships, but if her parents had been living proof that happiness was possible, she must believe in true love.

"Where are they now?"

Lanie's big eyes held his for only a second before she dropped her gaze to her lap, where her hands clutched the almost empty glass. She considered it for a moment before raising it to her lips and finishing the juice.

"My drink is empty, so I'd better get back to work. I

wouldn't want to disappoint my boss," she said, her smile almost apologetic as she rose.

As she stepped into the house, she turned around one more time. "Thank you, this was nice." Then she disappeared inside.

He watched through the glass door as she took her cleaning supplies and walked away, leaving him sitting outside alone. Except she hadn't retreated quickly enough this time.

The knowledge that Lanie believed in true love meant that she hadn't left him sitting here disappointed. Instead, he felt even more drawn to her than he had before.

CHAPTER 5

Mama Lita and Gabriela were already downstairs, but this morning, Lanie had a slow start. It was easy enough to figure out why. All last night, she'd kept replaying her conversation with Jordan.

She was all too aware that this would be the last day that she was on rotation to clean his villa. Even though she chided herself for it, she stared into the narrow mirror that hung on the back of her bedroom door to check how she looked.

The uniform she could do little about, but the way her hair was piled on top of her head in an unoriginal ponytail suddenly seemed like a bad idea.

Pulling the hair tie out again, she used her brush to smooth down her dark strands. While she usually preferred to leave her hair loose, letting it fall over her shoulders, that wasn't a good idea when cleaning. Instead, she twisted both sides backward to collect it all in a low bun. Turning back to the mirror, she could see that the twisted strands had the desired effect. Instead of appearing boring, her hair now added a bit of fun to her look.

Walking over to her nightstand, she opened the small pouch she'd packed full of little mementos. One of them was a hair clip that her mother had bought her on a trip they'd taken to Paris together. The beautiful pearls formed a small flower that was fun and elegant, yet subtle enough that she could wear it with her uniform without it looking ridiculous.

Refusing to reconsider the extra effort she was putting into her appearance today, she quickly left her room and went downstairs to grab a cup of coffee before she had to leave.

"You look nice," Mama Lita commented. The older woman was sitting at the table with her usual jelly toast.

"Thanks," Lanie said, trying to hide the flush she felt coloring her cheeks by turning to the coffeemaker.

"Oh, I love your hairpin," Gabriela chimed in. She'd been hidden behind the open refrigerator door but now emerged with a yogurt in hand.

Smiling, Lanie turned to her. "My mum bought it for me."

Surprise showed on Gabriela's face, and Lanie realized she hadn't spoken of her parents at all since she'd left home. Not once had she shared something about her family, and yesterday, she'd run away from Jordan after he'd asked her a simple question about them.

Apparently noticing Lanie's hesitation, Mama Lita jumped in. "It's pretty, but you girls need to be off to the pier to catch the boat for your shift."

"Darn, you're right," Gabriela said, grabbing a spoon and heading to the door to put her shoes on. "I guess I'll be eating on the way."

Lanie quickly poured some coffee in her travel mug and reluctantly followed her roommate. Despite her efforts with her hair this morning, she knew the source of her unease. After their conversation yesterday, it hadn't felt right to just walk away without sharing something about herself. She knew she had disappointed Jordan, and didn't that suck?

He'd been so open with her and had even told her about his hope to find true love. No other man had ever shared such a romantic notion with her, and she doubted she could look at him the same ever again. He'd always been attractive, but now she knew there was even more to him.

And yet, she'd walked away from him. Perhaps she could've talked about her parents, but she'd somehow become so used to not sharing anything in order to avoid slipping up that she'd reacted before considering whether she might make an exception.

As she sat next to Gabriela in the boat that brought them to Howler Island each morning, Lanie couldn't help but think that Jordan Dane seemed like the kind of man who was worth making exceptions for.

She'd escaped her old life to avoid being terrified of living. It wouldn't do to keep turning into the paranoid person she was well on her way to becoming. Wouldn't that be an even worse fate than being hunted and stalked? To have left everyone she loved behind, only to force herself into loneliness anyway because she was too afraid to let people in? It would be like letting Collin win.

She refused to become that type of person, always too afraid to make connections to the people around her. Here, she wanted to make herself a new home, and maybe Jordan's friendliness was what she needed to learn to trust again.

But when she entered his villa a little later, she found that his office chair was empty. Turning to the kitchen, she could almost feel her mood shifting inside her. The odd anticipation that had built during the golf cart ride from the welcome center was making way for disappointment. Maybe he had meetings again today and wouldn't be in. Then she wouldn't have the chance to make up for her rude retreat yesterday.

She seemed to always do the wrong thing around him.

A splash sounded from the open window, and Lanie's head instinctively turned toward the noise. Moving closer, she looked out to the pool, already expecting what she'd see. This time, she wasn't disappointed. Jordan was swimming in the pool behind the house. He must have just dived in because she could see the sun reflect in the water droplets in his hair.

She knew she should let him swim. She was here to clean, not to socialize. It was also his private home, and maybe he'd taken the day off and didn't want to be interrupted by an employee. And still, her feet carried her to the sliding doors that led to the deck. Turning to the right, she took a few steps and was now only a few meters away from the pool.

He hadn't noticed her yet. She could still walk away.

Jordan probably thought she was strange, anyway. After all, she'd walked away from him yesterday no more than thirty minutes after he'd just apologized for another instance in which it had actually been her who'd made the encounter awkward.

But she didn't turn around. Instead, she walked to the side of the pool and stood there, waiting for him to turn around and notice her.

The water surface rippled around him, his strokes even and strong. Despite the movement of the water, she could see the lean muscles of his back, and her eyes lingered on his form longer than she would have otherwise given herself permission to.

Then he turned around and spotted her. His face broke into a smile, and it was difficult not to feel like the most special person in the world even though Lanie had seen him smile at just about everyone like that.

Once, she'd seen him smile like this when one of the younger resort workers had come into his office, nervous and reluctant. Lanie had stood in the hallway and seen how Jordan had looked up from his computer and given the young man a smile and an encouraging nod.

Later, she'd learned that the boy had been worried about asking for a raise. Finding out the young man's girlfriend was pregnant, Jordan had arranged for the worker to start an accelerated apprenticeship instead of simply giving him a raise. It left all the workers who'd been in the break room to hear the young man recount his meeting with Jordan with even more respect for their boss.

Jordan's smiles were honest. They weren't the polite ones other people used but the type that showed he enjoyed being with people and helping them. And maybe that was even more attractive than thinking he reserved his happiness for only a few people.

When he swam to the end of the pool closest to her, Lanie blurted out the first thing that came to her mind.

"My parents are in Canada."

Clapping her mouth shut, she just looked at him. Why, oh why, was she unable to just be normal around him? A hello or good morning would have been normal, and those weren't difficult words. No, she, the woman who'd been trying to blend in and stay unnoticed, managed to keep drawing attention to all the ways she acted strangely.

Way to go, Lanie.

Blinking slowly, Jordan tilted his head for the briefest of moments, then he smiled again. "You must miss them."

And just like that, he'd said the perfect thing. He hadn't commented on her interrupting him or her running away from that very question the previous day, hadn't even asked her for more. No, Jordan was better than that. He tried to understand her and sensed that being separated from her parents was hard.

"I really do." With her eyes she tried to convey that she couldn't talk about this anymore, and his slow nod seemed to say he understood.

"I'd better get to it." She jabbed her thumb over her shoulder, pointing at the house.

"I'm glad you came out," he said, sounding truly pleased. "Good morning, Lanie."

"Good morning." Blushing, she turned around and began her work for the day.

She'd cleaned eight villas by the time her workday ended, and she felt sore. Not as bad as in the beginning, when her muscles had been untrained, but enough that a sigh escaped her lips when she slid onto the bench of the golf cart to drive back to the welcome center where she'd have to wait one hour for the boat to take the workers of the day shift back to Bocas.

Maybe she'd get lucky and someone had ordered a water cab and she could hitch a ride. Her earnings as a cleaner didn't allow unnecessary expenses, so she usually just waited for the official employee shuttle boat she could use for free.

When she arrived, she parked the cart and stored her tools in the shed designated for the cleaning supplies. Then, she made her way over to the marina office, where the temporary staff office was set up, but before she could open the door to step in, she heard her name being called from the opposite building.

Jordan was standing in the door to the welcome center where the construction crew had already finished their work for the day.

"Hello," she called back, unsure whether to approach him.

Had their brief interaction this morning changed anything? They spent time together yesterday, so maybe Jordan's friendliness meant he was interested in having an actual friendship that went beyond their work relationship. Perhaps he'd interpreted her coming to speak with him this morning as her signalling him that she wanted the same?

If only it were just friendship on her mind.

"You finished your shift? Are you going to wait for the staff boat?"

"That's the plan." She couldn't help the smile that formed on her lips. He looked like he was ready to model for the resort website rather than going about his workday.

Raising his arm to glance at his watch, Jordan waved for her to come over. "That's in an hour. Come on, we can kill some time by checking out how far they've gotten with the construction."

Not thinking twice, Lanie walked over.

Being with Jordan was strangely addictive despite her constant missteps. Her previous evasion had clearly been overboard, and the more practice she got with him, the better she'd get at navigating her new life. In fact, spending time with Jordan was probably the best kind of practice she could get since spending time with Mama Lita and Gabriela didn't mess with her presence of mind the same way as being with Jordan did.

Jordan's smile widened even more when he saw her move in his direction. She couldn't quite tell what the other emotion that briefly flitted over his face was. Was it surprise or was it something else?

The ongoing construction wasn't all that interesting to her, but she followed Jordan into the rooms that would be the new staff quarters anyway. While all she saw was debris and unfinished drywall, he seemed pleased with the progress, and being here was better than sitting around in the marina office by herself.

Since she'd kept to herself, she'd inadvertently given out the signal that she wasn't interested in socializing, even when it only involved random chit chat about the day's work. She was beginning to see how she'd stood in her own way of getting a new start here.

She'd thought she was keeping herself safe, but all she'd done was turn herself into an outsider, living alongside but not *with* her peers. She'd done exactly what she'd wanted to avoid back home, where she'd been afraid to pull people into her messy life. Except this was her home now, and she needed to start living her life again. And that involved making friends.

She turned to Jordan, who was just showing her where the new bath and change rooms would be. "It'll be good to have the extra showers. At Mama Lita's house, Gabriela and I are sharing one, so one of us usually ends up eating dinner in their uniform."

"At least you get to eat Mama Lita's cooking." Jordan grinned. "I miss her meals. I think I'd trade my shower to be able to have someone cook for me."

"I'm not a great cook myself. The food is amazing, but I swear, if I stay living with her, I'll be so round you'll soon confuse me for a coconut."

"Hardly." His voice was slightly gruff, but he turned away quickly, and she couldn't read his expression.

They continued their light banter while Jordan quickly checked whether the electrical outlets were working. It was good to have someone to talk with, and it dawned on her how lonely she'd become despite her amazing housemates.

Luckily, Gabriela had ignored Lanie's standoffish behavior from the start. If Mama Lita saw her as worth saving, Gabriela had said once, then surely, she must be a good person. So, whenever Gabriela was around, she included Lanie, and since they were roommates, they often shared the boat ride to and from the island, which was a good start.

But despite her roommate's welcoming attitude, it still left Lanie with few people to hang out with. If Jordan was willing to have her trail after him, she might as well begin her efforts toward becoming an ingrained part of the Howler Island community right here and now.

She was here to stay, after all.

Now all she had to do was stop noticing the way his jeans hugged his butt, and they could end up squarely in the friends category.

Picturing the muscles she knew were hidden underneath his shirt and fantasizing about the way his skin was tanned from swimming in his pool should also stop. Well, she'd stop it right after they were finished with their tour. It wasn't as if she could help it.

Unfortunately, Jordan seemed pleased with everything he'd checked, and he started walking again, leaving her to follow him back to the front of the building.

As if they had a life of their own, her eyes scanned his body while he leaned down to pick up an empty discarded water bottle, throwing it in one of the trash cans. It was like they were glued to him.

Yes, Jordan Dane was magnetic, all right. But it wasn't just his personality.

* * *

She was checking him out. There was no question about it, and it excited him more than he should allow it to.

This woman was testing his control in ways he'd never expected. Her beauty was something any straight guy would have noticed, her big eyes meant to enchant men, but it was her efforts to let him in and share something about herself this morning, when he could sense that it had been a big step for her, that had made him call her name earlier.

Maybe it was the random sparks of longing he'd noticed when she looked out to the ocean that made him want to know what her life was like outside the nine hours each day that she spent at the resort. With each passing day this week, she'd looked more as if she wanted to be here, wanted to allow herself the right to step out of her well-tended shell and live her life.

Or maybe it was the moments when he sensed she was as affected by him as he was by her. He doubted she realized that he'd caught her eyes traveling over his body this morning when he'd been in the pool. It had all but fried the cells in his brain that knew better than to lust after a woman working for him.

Whatever it was, he wanted this woman.

Throwing the bottle one of the construction workers must have dropped on the ground into the garbage, Jordan frantically tried to recall that it wasn't a good idea to cross that line with her. He was her boss. It was unethical. Though he'd been pestered more than once that he needed to notice the beautiful women who worked here. Except none of them had ever tempted him to ignore the fact that his position might present an undue influence on a woman whom he wanted to proposition.

The other reason was Lanie herself. She was definitely checking him out, but he'd also seen her retreat faster than a skittish vine snake. However much her looks were telling him she was as interested as he was, there was no way he'd risk pushing her into something she might not actually want. Looking differed from acting, after all.

Today, she looked a little different, and it hadn't taken him long to pinpoint that it was her hair. Instead of a severe ponytail, she'd done something else with it, and for whatever reason, that little change gave him hope that her interested looks meant more.

Her lips were shiny from her tongue running over them, and watching her absent-minded movement made him want to pull her against him until he could feel the softness of her mouth. But he had no right to do that.

There was one way he might solve his conundrum. It wasn't perfect, but he was willing to take a risk if it meant that she might say yes and truly mean it.

"Lanie, I need to ask you something, and you need to know that whatever answer you give me, I will respect it completely. There is absolutely no wrong thing to say here, and I promise your answer won't change a thing."

Worry widened her eyes, and he almost drew back. Maybe he'd completely miscalculated. Maybe she wasn't interested. But he'd begun now, so he decided to leave it up to her. He'd simply be honest about his interest. It was a risk, but Lanie was worth taking it.

"I'm interested in you, Lanie. Interested in a romantic sense, but I know that with my being your boss, you might find yourself uncomfortable about it. I promise you, if you say you're not interested, I will never mention it again and I will make sure to give you space and professional respect and nothing more."

He knew he should leave it at that, but now that he'd started talking, he couldn't stop himself. "I truly mean that I will respect your refusal completely, but Lanie, if you're interested too, then please tell me because there is nothing I would rather do right now than kiss you."

He stayed in place, not moving toward her in the way he wanted to. He wanted to take her hand, stroke her cheek, but he didn't. She needed to know he'd respect her boundaries. She needed to know she could walk away right now.

He kept his eyes on her face, closely monitoring her reaction. If her worried look would turn into regret, or worse, fear, he'd step back even further. He'd tell Logan what he'd said to her and make sure that his friend would assure Lanie that she could turn to someone else if she felt uncomfortable working for Jordan. That her job was safe.

But instead of showing regret or fear, Lanie's pupils widened, and she leaned toward him. Her tongue darted to her lips again as if her subconscious was already preparing for the kiss he'd promised her.

Still, it wasn't enough. He needed for her to say it. He needed for her to confirm that she wanted this too, that he wasn't overstepping. Nothing less than her clearly spoken consent would be enough right now.

He wanted to prompt her, to ask her to tell him what she was thinking. The seconds she took to respond felt like hours were stretching out between them. But he didn't push her. He couldn't. If he got to kiss her, he wanted it to be the right thing, no doubt lingering that he was imposing himself on her.

"I'm interested." Her voice was a whisper, and it sounded almost as if she'd said the words without meaning to.

"I can't kiss you if I'm not absolutely sure that you're certain you want it too, Lanie." Jordan could hear the desperation in his own voice. Squashing the urgency he felt, he measured his tone more carefully. If she needed time to decide, then she'd get it. "You don't need to make up your mind now, if you don't want to. I promise you that. I will honor your words. But when you decide, I need to know if I have your consent. Nothing less than that will be enough, okay?"

He looked at her, trying to convey his resolve even while everything in him longed to press his lips against hers.

She blinked once, her brows drawing together, and the next thing he knew, she was leaning against him, her momentum propelling him backward a step.

"I do," she breathed. "I want you to kiss me."

Everything inside him screamed success, but he willed his hands to be gentle, not to rush her. With her already pressed against him, she'd feel his body's reaction, and still, he cradled her face in his hands, leaning back slightly to look at her.

"You're sure?"

This time, her answer was louder, no longer a whispered declaration but a confident assertion. "Yes. Kiss me, Jordan."

And he did. Pressing his lips against hers, his earlier restraint dissolved. His hand slid down her back, pressing her even closer against him as his tongue darted out to taste her.

She tasted like sunshine. Like happiness. Whatever worries she battled with, none of them were part of this kiss. This was Lanie in her purest form, a happy, open, giving woman whose lips were simultaneously soft and demanding.

With some mental effort, he pulled his left hand from her back and reached to the side, opening the door that led into his office. A tarp still covered the desk to protect the wood from construction debris. Stumbling back, with Lanie clinging to him, he quickly grabbed the plastic material and ripped it away. Then his hand slid back around Lanie and grabbed her butt. Lifting her, he turned them around until she sat on the desk, her legs tangled around him in a way that made him fight the urge to grind against her.

Maybe he would have succeeded, but then Lanie let out a low whine. "Jordan, I need you closer." With that, nothing could have stopped him from pressing more tightly against her, finding the friction they were both seeking.

Her hands roved up his neck, tangling in his hair and holding his face close to hers. His lips teased hers to open until he could feel her breath hot against his.

"Fuck." He groaned. Her eyes opened, and Jordan could see the same emotions he was feeling reflected back to him. Surprise, hunger, need. He dove back into the kiss, not knowing how he'd ever stop.

His hands fisted in her hair, and her legs wrapped around his waist. They clung to each other in a frenzied desperation. Her breathing was just as labored as his. Her urgency was the same as his. And every move she made just stoked the fire that was burning rampant inside him.

Until a bell quietly rang and Lanie stiffened in his arms. Immediately, he stepped back a small step, his body protesting the loss of contact, hating to leave the heat behind.

"I have to go," she said, and before he could argue, she'd already jumped off the desk, smoothing down her skirt as she walked to the door.

His brain only now processed what Lanie must have realized immediately. What he'd heard was the bell that announced the boat that shuttled the staff members to Bocas Town where most of them lived.

Even as he wanted to tell her he'd give her a ride himself, she'd already stepped out the door, calling a goodbye over her shoulder.

CHAPTER 6

"Wait for me," Lanie called, pulling the dangling hair clip out of her hair.

Hastily, she made her way down the dock to catch the water taxi which was already filled with employees eager to get home after their shifts. It was the last boat for the day, and she couldn't afford to miss it.

When she got close, Gabriela was holding out her hand, her expression intrigued as she took in Lanie's ruffled hair and blouse. Lanie cursed herself for not straightening up, but if she'd done that, she may have missed the boat.

How had she let herself get so carried away?

She'd lost track of time entirely, only the bell of the boat cutting through her lust-filled haze.

She took a seat next to Gabriela on the crowded bench, not sure what she should tell her friend but knowing she'd better think of something fast.

"I thought your shift ended early?" Gabriela prompted. "I figured you caught a ride with another boat when you weren't in the marina office."

Lanie suppressed a sigh. She wanted to tell the truth, but that didn't seem like a viable option. While she truly despised the constant lying, she also didn't want to get Jordan in any trouble. His outright demand for her spoken consent had made it obvious that he wasn't only a gentleman but was also painfully aware of the HR nightmare that kissing an employee could mean for him.

When Gabriela raised an eyebrow, obviously ready to start an inquisition if Lanie didn't explain herself, she quickly resigned herself to lying once again. "No, you're right, my shift ended a while ago. I just forgot something and had to look for it."

"What was it?" Gabriela asked curiously, looking Lanie up and down.

Her sanity? "My hair clip."

"Oh, no, the one your mother gave you?" The concern in her friend's face touched Lanie. They may be new friends, but Gabriela obviously cared enough for her to have realized that losing that hair clip would have hurt Lanie badly.

"Yes, that one," Lanie said and pulled it out of her pocket to show Gabriela. "But I found it."

It felt good to know that at least this tiny detail, how much it meant to her to have something that linked her to her family, was something she could share with her housemate. She wanted to stick to her new resolution to allow her new friends in. Though, perhaps she'd taken that a bit too literally with Jordan. Heat rising to her cheeks, she tried to dispel the lingering feeling of his lips on hers so she could concentrate on the conversation.

Quickly, she tucked the clip back into her pocket, not wanting to risk the wind blowing it away. The boat had taken off and was now leaving the small harbor of the resort to speed across the water toward the bigger island where Bocas Town and their house waited for them.

"That explains why you look so mussed up." Gabriela laughed. "I thought you got yourself a secret boyfriend." She waggled her eyebrows suggestively.

Lanie forced herself to grin. "I'll leave the hot resort guests to you."

They both knew neither of them would touch a resort guest. Gabriela might joke and flirt a bit, but like Lanie, she depended on this job. Neither of them would risk breaking any of the resort rules. Like the one about no fraternizing with the guests. Of course, Lanie was sure there was also an unwritten rule about making out with the boss.

She suppressed her groan.

She knew she'd have to talk to him. Except getting close enough to speak with Jordan might be dangerous. The man was like a magnet for her. Perhaps she could just call him? Except that would be even more awkward.

This time, she couldn't suppress her sigh. She needed to suck it up and go tell him that today had been a mistake and that they needed to keep a professional relationship. Except she wouldn't use that word. Relationship.

They needed to keep a professional distance. Yes, that was better. Distance was exactly what she needed. Even if it wasn't what she wanted.

The way his tongue had darted over her lower lip as he sucked on it had sent electricity through her entire body, and she was fairly certain she could still feel some of the sparks erupt throughout her body.

On Monday, she'd talk to him.

With a jerk, the small boat sidled against the private pier the resort kept in Bocas, and Lanie followed Gabriela down the wooden dock and through the reception area until they stood on the busy main street.

"Are you up for a cocktail tonight?" Gabriela asked.

She wanted to say no, that she needed time to figure out what had gotten into her today, that she needed to sit down and remind herself of all the reasons she couldn't make mistakes, but the thought of sitting in her room with the images from *before* flitting through her mind until she ended up with nightmares again didn't appeal to her in the least. Thus, she nodded.

A cocktail was a frivolous expense she hadn't thought of twice when she'd had a good paying job in marketing, but now that she worked with a tight budget, it was a treat she rarely indulged in. Today seemed like she deserved something with a kick, though.

They walked the twenty minutes home to shower and change. The thought that once the resort had installed the new employee bathing and changing rooms, they'd be able to wash up and put on fresh clothes before going home was nice. They'd even be able to go out immediately after work if they wanted to, or she could get groceries and run errands without being in her maid's uniform, something she avoided for now.

It wasn't that she was embarrassed about her position. She was thankful for her job, and she'd never been spoken down to, but after cleaning a number of bathrooms, it just didn't feel right to handle fresh produce before taking a nice long shower.

When they arrived at Mama Lita's house, the door stood slightly ajar.

"Mama Lita?" Gabriela called as they entered, but the older woman didn't answer. Lanie could feel goosebumps build on her skin. An unlocked door, no one home. It felt too familiar.

"Huh, she must have gone over to chat with the neighbors and didn't close the door properly," Gabriela murmured.

Lanie nodded, trying to dispel the cold. "Does she do that often?"

"Not really, but it happens occasionally. The lock on this door is useless, anyway, if someone wanted to break in."

Her friend's assurance didn't feel particularly reassuring. Still, Lanie tried to rein in her growing panic. If Gabriela wasn't worried, she probably shouldn't allow herself to freak out just yet. On the other hand, she knew all too well that ignoring such subtle signs that something was wrong could end badly.

"Just to be sure, let's do a quick check of the house together, okay?"

"Why not?" Gabriela shrugged, though Lanie didn't miss the skeptical look that had flashed across the other woman's face.

With Gabriela's agreement, they did a walk-through of the house, finding everything as it should be, and Lanie finally relaxed. At some point, she might stop feeling like she needed to control her environment so carefully, but until then, she was glad she wasn't alone in the house.

* * *

A full minute after Lanie left, Jordan was still standing in his office, staring at the door she'd gone through, when his phone buzzed in his pocket.

"Should I pick you up at your villa?" Logan's voice sounded through the speaker.

Jordan had all but forgotten that they'd agreed to go out for some beers tonight.

"I'm at the welcome center, actually, so we can just meet here."

When he'd asked Logan to hang out a couple of days ago, he'd hoped his friend might be able to help him figure out how to approach dating. Now he'd have to do his best not to let slip just how far he'd thrown himself out there just now.

"Give me fifteen minutes and I'll meet you there."

Ten minutes later, Logan arrived with a wide grin. "Let's go. Jane is still at the Aualotta Relief compound, probably caught up in her research again, so you're saving her from being dragged home before she's finished." His friend's deep laugh told Jordan that he probably shouldn't ask just how often Logan dragged his wife home from her work. Not that he believed for a second that Jane truly minded.

As they took the boat over to the bigger island, Logan told Jordan how Jane was trying to get ahead on a new research report she was writing. Jordan let him talk, his own thoughts still revolving around Lanie's kiss and the way she'd walked off.

Had she only wanted to catch the boat, or had she been relieved to be interrupted before things got too far?

He had no idea how far they would have gone if it hadn't been for that damned bell. He certainly wouldn't mind taking things further with her, but Lanie was so reserved that he knew he'd have to give her time to warm up to the idea of something more between them.

At least he was certain she'd wanted the kiss. Then again, she kept pulling back at unexpected times, and he'd need to be very careful not to scare her away. Because he wanted her even more now that he'd had a taste of her. She was intriguing, and he wanted to figure out what had brought her here. Something inside him had responded to her from the minute he'd first met her.

As Logan navigated their small boat toward the pier of the pub they always went to when Logan was around, Jordan decided it was worth the risk. The next time he saw Lanie, he'd talk to her and figure out if she was interested in going on an actual date.

"We haven't had a beer at the pub in ages," Logan commented as he tied the boat to the metal ring screwed into the pier.

Jordan looked up, surprised that they'd already arrived. "True, we haven't."

Logan headed to one of the free tables that stood on the adjacent back deck overlooking the water. It was early enough for the water to still be busy with tourists and locals on their boats, and the pub was just starting to fill with people.

Later, it would grow more crowded as the fishermen and tour guides called an end to their workday. Tourists usually favored the fancier bars along the main street where they could drink import beers and fancy cocktails, but the pub never lacked local patrons.

A server came over, greeting them by name, and they

ordered their beers.

"So," Logan began. "Are you finally going to tell me why you took several months off work to travel?"

It was an answer Jordan had known he'd have to get into, eventually. Until now, he'd only given his best friend the excuse that he'd needed to get away from the island to figure out if he had made the right choice by staying here when everyone else had moved away and on to other things. It wasn't a lie, and perhaps it was enough of a reason on its own, but while Jordan might prefer to keep ignoring his other motivation for leaving, Logan knew him too well to accept that it was the only reason.

"Yeah, I should. You know how much I appreciate that you gave me that leave, right?"

Logan nodded. "Worked out for me."

The lucky coincidence that Logan had met Jane during his absence had meant Jordan had gotten away with little scrutiny regarding his disappearance.

Women could be quite distracting. Jordan would know.

"You know I haven't had any contact with my father. After he left my mother when she got pregnant, I never heard a word from him. Only when Mom died, and she told me he'd been paying her money every year, did I even know that he hadn't ignored my existence completely." Like everyone else, Jordan had assumed his mother was just scraping by with her income. She'd certainly always had them living on a tight budget.

When she'd gotten so sick that it was clear that she'd pass away soon, she'd told Jordan that he was going to inherit all the money his father had paid her over the years. She'd put it all into a fund to pay for his education, never to be touched. It had been a shock, and Jordan had wanted nothing to do with the money, which is why he'd given it to his friends so they could start their companies.

Since Logan had received more than half of that money to start Graw Resorts, he was one of the very few people who knew this part of Jordan's story.

Nodding, Logan waited for Jordan to get on with his explanation.

"Well, I didn't hear a word from him until last year. And even then, it wasn't really from him. His lawyer wrote to me, telling me my father had died." He could remember that day well. He hadn't thought he had any feelings for the man, and that had held true. There had been no grief, no regret over a missed opportunity, nothing. And still, Jordan had wandered down to the beach that evening, staring at the water and wondering how much the man he'd never met had shaped his life.

"Good riddance," Logan murmured, and Jordan gave him a crooked grin.

"That's right. Anyway, I didn't care about the man, and the only reason the lawyer called was because it was a formality for him to check off his list. No personal notes or anything. I told him I wanted nothing to do with the estate and that was that. Except, I guess it made me wonder whether I stayed on the island because he'd left it. It sounds messed up, but it just started to bug me. So, I decided to go on a trip and see what it was like to leave Howler Island behind."

"Huh." Logan's noncommittal grunt almost made Jordan laugh, but then Logan looked up, making eye contact. "So, what did you figure out when you left?"

Now Jordan smiled. "For one, that my best friend is a solid guy to step up for me like that. Also, that Howler Island will always be my home, and my job as manager at the resort is the perfect fit for me. Traveling was great, and I'm glad I got the chance, but this is where I'm going to stay. I'm honestly not sure if part of me stayed here as some sort of rebellion when I was younger, but now I'm here just because it's where I want to live."

"Well, I won't complain. It's good to have family

together." Logan's words reflected Jordan's own feelings.

Equally pleased that his best friend was also back to Howler Island, Jordan raised his beer, and they clinked their glasses together.

For the next little while, they moved on to more casual chit chat about the resort, Logan's other businesses, and the expanding tourism industry of the area. It was only when Jordan noticed two women enter the pub that his thoughts returned to his latest obsession. At first, he wasn't sure, but when the two women came out to the back deck where he and Logan were sitting, he realized that the curvy woman in the casual green dress was really Lanie.

"Who are you looking at?"

Jordan quickly looked back at Logan, who was grinning at him.

"I know that look. You're seeing someone you like." Logan swiveled in his chair, trying to figure out whom Jordan had spotted. After a few seconds, Logan turned around again, his eyes wide.

"Gabriela? I didn't think you guys ever went beyond being friends."

Quickly, Jordan shook his head. "You know I don't date employees." Except he'd kissed one today.

"And that's exactly what I want to hear as your boss, but

as your friend, I know you've been single for way too long. I'm not saying you should hook up with any of the women working at the resort, but if you're honestly interested in dating someone, we could definitely work something out. You're no longer alone on the island to manage the place. Now that I'm back, whoever you date would have someone else to turn to."

Jordan had had the same idea, though he knew it was a flawed plan. Everyone knew they were good friends, which would defeat the purpose of having a neutral party involved to mediate things and make sure there was no undue pressure. Still, he wanted to get to know Lanie.

He watched as she and Gabriela took a table on the other side of the deck, unaware that he was watching them. She looked as pretty as always, though seeing her in something other than her uniform gave him a thrill. Was this what she'd look like if they went on a date together?

Logan turned around, following Jordan's gaze again. Clearly, Jordan was being much too obvious.

"Okay, if you're not staring at Gabriela, then who is the woman with her? She looks kind of familiar. Does she work for us, too?"

"Yeah. Her name is Lanie. And as for the HR issue, I think we need to figure out a better plan."

Now Logan gave him a measuring look, his grin changing into a serious expression. "How so?"

"I kissed her. Well, she kissed me, I think. But whatever the case, you may be the boss, but you're also my best friend, so you're hardly a neutral party she could turn to if she had concerns."

"I see." The contemplative look on Logan's face told Jordan his friend was taking his concerns quite seriously. "I'll call my headquarters tomorrow and work something out, but I'm going to need to know more, man. You guys kissed? When did this happen, and how do I only hear about this now?"

Logan was in boss mode now, and Jordan couldn't help but grin at his friend. This was what he liked best about Logan. The guy had ethics and was business savvy besides being loyal to the bone.

"It happened about twenty minutes before we met tonight. I would've told you, but I'm still figuring out what my next step is."

"Next step?"

Jordan nodded. "Yeah. I'm going to ask her out."

"Sounds to me like you've already figured out your next step." Now it was Logan's turn to grin.

Jordan suppressed a groan. "I wouldn't say that. More

like I know what I want, but getting there is still up in the air."

Logan's laughter wasn't helpful in the least, and Jordan wondered whether punching him might help wipe that amused look off his friend's face.

"Ever considered asking her?" Logan continued being unhelpful.

"No shit." Logan was right, the smug bastard. Except he could hardly walk up to Lanie and ask her out while Gabriela was sitting next to her. That was a safe way to make sure the entire staff would know his no-dating rule had blown up in his face. He wasn't prepared for the awkwardness that would cause.

"I need to catch her alone."

Logan's eyebrows rose. "So that's your plan to make sure you don't come across as a pervy predator?"

This time, Jordan did punch his friend, though he aimed at Logan's shoulder, and the guy had the audacity to laugh.

"You know, you're not being helpful in the least," Jordan accused.

"Looks like you have to act like a big boy and actually convince her by yourself."

That was exactly his intention, and while he and Logan

ordered another round of beers, his eyes kept straying over to Lanie, an idea forming in his mind.

Eventually, Logan gave Jane a call, who had offered to come pick them up. They would leave Logan's boat here, where one of the resort workers would take it over the next day.

Jane's arrival was marked by the shocked gasp of a woman a few tables over who sat closest to the side of the pier. Apparently, the woman had noticed Jane's distracted appearance and the way Logan's wife was steering her boat directly at the pier rather than sidling up against it.

Logan jumped up. "Jane!"

His call was enough to get her attention, and realizing how close to the pier she was, Jane quickly slowed her approach and managed to bump against the tires that had been attached to the side of the dock with minimal force.

"Dear lord, woman," Logan called to his wife, though it was clear from his tone that he was more teasing than actually upset. "If you can't get your academic head to focus on the real world at least occasionally, I think I'd be safer taking the boat home myself, a couple of beers or not."

Jane's consternated expression was pure gold, and Jordan worked hard not to grin.

"I'm thinking about the real world, thank you very

much. I'm a scientist, not a psychic. And the day you take a boat drunk will be the day I'll have you run all the manual fecal tests for the monkey dung."

While Logan and Jane kept talking, Jordan glanced over his shoulder and met Lanie's eyes. Obviously, Jane's arrival had caught her attention as well. He noticed she was sitting alone, Gabriela nowhere in sight, so he muttered an excuse to Logan and Jane and walked over to her table.

"Hey," she said, sounding unsure of what to say beyond the greeting.

"Are you enjoying your evening?" It was hardly the best start to their conversation, but jumping in with *Hey, I liked our kiss earlier, let's go on a date* didn't seem like the best plan, either.

"Yes, I'm here with Gabriela." Lanie looked over to the restrooms as if Gabriela could appear at any moment, which might very well be true. It was time to get to the point.

"Would you be free tomorrow? I think it'd be good to talk. Maybe I could come to Bocas and meet you here."

To his surprise, Lanie nodded immediately. "I was going to come talk to you on Monday, but this might be better."

After they'd agreed on a time, Jordan quickly walked back to Logan and Jane, who were both watching him.

When he climbed into the boat, he saw Gabriela emerge from the bathroom. Would Lanie tell her friend what had happened? He doubted it, though surprisingly, he found himself liking the idea that Lanie might want to share that she'd kissed him.

She wanted to talk to him, too. But why? Had she decided that their kiss had been a mistake, or was she open to seeing him again? Even before he made it back to his villa, Jordan knew he wouldn't get any sleep tonight.

CHAPTER 7

Lanie stood in the little park Jordan had suggested as a meeting spot yesterday, and she couldn't help the nervous flutters in her stomach.

The kiss yesterday had been amazing.

It had been everything a kiss should be, but it also meant she'd broken all of her rules. He was the one person here who was more likely than anyone else to figure out that she wasn't using her real name, and she'd gone and kissed him.

Last night, though, as she'd been alone in her bed, all she'd been able to think about had been the feel of Jordan's body pressed against hers. He'd kissed her with a fervor she hadn't experienced since . . . well, never. During her university years, she'd certainly had a few impassioned make-out sessions, but nothing could compare to being kissed by a man like Jordan. Just like his personality was open and outgoing, his kiss had felt like he was giving her all of him. And she wanted to keep taking.

Jordan was the type of man she'd dreamed of meeting before. He was everything she admired. Fun, outgoing, committed to his work. Except dreaming up a person could never compare to the real thing. Her daydreams didn't come close to the excited feeling of meeting someone who so perfectly encapsulated everything you admired and desired.

She paced toward the water. She hardly knew him. It was ridiculous to let her feelings run away with her like that. She wasn't a lovesick teenager, and yet, being rational didn't make Jordan appeal to her any less. He was hard-working, ethical, and kind.

The boats out on the water were gently swaying in the wind, a stark contrast to the storm of emotions inside her. While most of the waterfront was lined with restaurants, bars, and tourist shops that offered boat tours and diving expeditions, the park had carved out a bit of space for people to look over the glistening water to the lush islands further out.

She had to walk past here every morning to catch the boat to Howler Island, but it was usually in the afternoons, on her way home, that she paused here to take in the view. Sure, the view of the various islands was even more impressive on the boat, but here she could be alone and get lost in her thoughts.

She wanted to make this her home. It hadn't been part of her plan before. But now, staying here felt less like being exiled and more like a possibility.

It wasn't just yesterday that she'd begun thinking like this, but the kiss she'd shared with Jordan had reminded her that there was more to life than finding a job and a place to live. She wanted a real home, and one day, she wanted to fall in love and share her life with someone. That it was her boss who tempted her more than any other man ever had was a slight complication, but maybe she needed to let go of some of the paranoia that still clung to her and embrace a little more of her old self.

When she turned away from the water, she caught sight of Jordan walking toward her. His face showed his signature easygoing smile, and he lifted a hand to wave at her casually. She'd been like that before. Her best friend Mona had always called her Lori-Sunshine. Now she was standing in a Caribbean paradise, and she wanted some of that sunshine back, so she lifted her hand in return and smiled at Jordan.

Today, she'd allow herself to just live as if this were the

only life she had. She'd embrace her new life and allow herself to feel the sunshine and possibilities. Whether it was that she was burned out from pretending or that she just couldn't hold on to being afraid anymore, she needed a day to let go of the stress.

"You look very nice." Jordan greeted her, still smiling.

Pleased with her decision, Lanie dipped into a playful curtsy. "Well, thank you. So do you."

Jordan laughed and offered her his arm. "I had an idea, but only if you're up for it."

Whatever endorphins yesterday's kiss had released, right now, they told Lanie to just go with it. "What are you thinking?"

"Well, from what I understand, you just arrived here when you got the job at the resort, so I figure you probably haven't had the chance to do any of the touristy things yet. I was thinking we could take the day, and I'll show you some of the best places this area has to offer."

He looked so excited that Lanie wanted to laugh, and after a moment, she just gave in to it. Giggling, she nodded. "I'd like that."

Laughing too, Jordan gave her a mock skeptical glance. "Was I being funny?"

Shaking her head, Lanie got herself back under

control. "It's just that I expected more of a serious conversation today, not a date, but I'd love to see the area, so if you're offering to be my tour guide, then I'm more than happy to spend the day with you." If she was throwing caution to the wind today, she might as well make it worthwhile, and Jordan's delighted expression was enough to confirm that spending the day with him would be anything but a chore.

"We definitely need to talk, but first, let's walk to my boat so I can show you the dolphins."

It was hard to argue when she was getting the chance to see dolphins, so Lanie let Jordan lead her to a private dock that was only a few spots down from that of the resort. Bocas was small enough that there was a good chance someone would see them together, but if Jordan didn't mind, neither did she.

While he steered them out onto the water, Jordan explained that his boat was a bass boat. Lanie's best guess was that it was about twenty feet long, and unlike the re-purposed fishing boat she was used to taking to Howler Island, his boat was lower to the water and without a roof. It was also a lot faster, and instead of talking, they allowed the wind to whip around them in a nice relief from the blistering sun. It was just past eleven, and the temperatures were inching upward to reach their midday peak soon.

With the wind on the open water tugging at her clothes, Lanie was glad that she hadn't put on a dress, instead wearing a pair of Capri pants she'd bought in the local general store paired with a simple white blouse she'd brought with her when she'd come here.

Eventually, Jordan slowed the boat. They were sitting side by side, the nearest island reaching out of the water to their right, the water around it glistening in the sunlight. Even though they weren't quite touching, she could feel Jordan's body beside her. He was close enough that her senses picked up each of his movements. Instead of looking at him, though, she stalled, suddenly nervous.

Turning away from him, she looked toward the distant island. They were too far away to see whether anyone was tanning on the sandy beach she could make out in the distance, but it was obvious that it was as beautiful there as the beaches on Howler Island. Not that Lanie had gotten the chance to tan or swim there yet.

"Look over there," Jordan said suddenly, drawing her attention to the other side of the boat.

At first, all Lanie could see was the way the sun was glistening in the small ripples that still showed on the water's surface from their boat, but after a moment, a gray fin reached out of the water in a graceful bow.

"That's one of the bottlenose dolphins that live here," Jordan said before turning to look at her with a more serious expression. "Their population is decreasing, but they aren't considered a threatened population just yet. Unfortunately, some people who operate boats around here aren't skilled or care too little, and dolphins sometimes get injured. I'm very careful when coming this way, but boat traffic is getting busier, and soon we'll have to consider some sort of regulation on a local level. They are too beautiful to not protect."

The sad fact that even here in this absolute paradise, people were putting other species in danger momentarily marred the beauty of the moment. When another dolphin shot out of the water, though, body flying into the air, Lanie couldn't hold on to the sentimental feeling. The sheer wonder of seeing such an incredible animal in the wild was too thrilling, and for the next little while, all they did was watch the pod as they passed by them.

As the animals' amazing strength and energy took her in, Lanie promised herself to look up what conservation initiatives existed and make up for being yet another tourist coming here into the dolphins' domain. If she was planning on making this her home, she was responsible for not letting those who lived here before her suffer for it.

Once the pod had passed, Jordan started the boat's engine again, and they made their way to the island Lanie had admired earlier.

"They have a small restaurant and a nice beach here. I thought we could get something to eat for lunch and then walk for a bit?" Jordan looked so hopeful that Lanie knew her own face was breaking into yet another smile. Between the dolphins and her decision to just choose happiness for the day, she felt so much lighter and was glad she could share the day with Jordan. She certainly hadn't smiled this much since she'd arrived in Bocas.

"I'd like that." And she meant it. It was nearly impossible to linger on anything depressing when she was around Jordan, and she wasn't ready to start worrying again just yet. Plus, the thought of eating out felt like a treat.

"What kind of food do they have?" Unfortunately, she had to be very careful about frivolous expenses, but like the cocktail yesterday, this would be worth the additional shift she'd have to take on.

While Mama Lita often cooked for Gabriela and her, those were also the only actual meals Lanie had been eating since she arrived. Mama Lita's cooking was hardy and primarily featured beans and rice. Lanie couldn't deny that she craved some variety, but since she was an abysmal cook, it was either taking advantage of her fairy godmother's gracious hospitality or sticking with sandwiches and cereal.

"They've got curry, burgers, salads, and paninis, but the curry is definitely the best. Honestly, though, the main reason you've got to eat there is the dessert. They do all kinds of cool stuff with cacao." Jordan's enthusiasm sounded like that of a young boy who was about to get a special treat, and Lanie found herself matching his expression.

By the time Jordan secured his boat and they walked from the pier to the restaurant, Lanie's mouth was positively watering. It was obvious that Jordan was a big fan of the kitchen here, and Lanie had to wonder what cook had managed to inspire such passion in a man.

Once they picked a table, it became obvious that even if the food wasn't as good as Jordan promised, she'd like this place. The view was absolutely stunning.

Underneath them, a nearly empty sandy beach reached in both directions. The low-hanging palm trees obstructed the view of any other buildings, though Lanie could just make out a surfing hut further down the beach. It also helped that a fan pointed almost directly at their table, which meant Lanie could admire the midday sun shining over the water without suffering from the smoldering heat.

So far, they'd talked little, enjoying the boat ride and the dolphins, but now that they were seated across from each other, neither of them having picked up the menu yet, Lanie couldn't hold on to the lightness of the past hour. She could see in Jordan's expression that he was about to bring up the kiss, and as much as she simply wanted to go on with their day, pretending that this was a simple first date, she also knew she had to give him the chance to say what he needed to. Not only was he her boss, but she needed to know what he was thinking about her.

"I'm glad you agreed to meet me today, Lanie," Jordan began, and suddenly, Lanie couldn't help but notice that below his easygoing smile, Jordan's face held angular lines that were usually obscured by the laugh marks around his lips and eyes.

She knew he was in his early thirties, but when he laughed, he looked slightly younger. Now that he wasn't joking but looking at her with a serious expression, he looked his age, and as much as she would have doubted it before, he looked even more handsome. Confident, serious, and determined.

A nervous tingle ran down her spine. It seemed that Jordan hadn't gotten the memo that today wasn't supposed to be serious, that it was about enjoying life and finding yourself again. And still, another feeling lower in her belly told her she liked the way he was looking at her. Like he was intent on having this conversation because the kiss had mattered.

"I'm glad we kissed yesterday, and I need you to know that I've informed Logan Graw, my boss, about it. In case you feel that there is any undue pressure because I'm your boss, you need to know that you can turn to the Graw Resorts headquarters. Since Logan is my friend, he will set something up so you won't have to deal with him either, if you don't want to, though I promise you that Logan is absolutely trustworthy and would handle any concerns you might bring to him with utmost care."

Lanie couldn't help her smile return. "And do you plan on placing any undue pressure on me? Because as far as I can tell, our kiss yesterday was mutual."

She didn't give him enough time to respond before continuing. Her voice was more serious this time because he needed to know that she appreciated that he did everything properly to avoid making her feel uncomfortable in any way. It was what every employee should expect, what every woman should expect, and yet his forthright approach stood out.

"Jordan, I appreciate this, and I will be mindful of it, but I'm here because I want to be, not because I feel pressured. And I kissed you because I wanted to. You don't need to worry about that. If I have any concerns in the future, I'll come to you first and share them with you before I would need to go to headquarters. Still, I appreciate that you're doing everything by the book."

Now his grin reappeared. "So, you want to be here, huh?"

She doubted he could see the flush creep up her cheeks since she was already flushed from the temperature, but she couldn't help feeling flustered because she truly did want to be here . . . and wasn't that thrilling? She wanted to spend more time with Jordan, wanted to get to know him better, wanted to learn more about his childhood growing up here.

It was the one thing she'd avoided in the past month, but today, she just couldn't keep pretending that she didn't long for a deeper conversation, a deeper connection to not just anybody but to Jordan.

"I do. And I also want food. How about we order something?" Deflecting was better than trying to tackle the overwhelming feelings rushing through her right now. She'd have to sort through those when she was alone.

Jordan ordered the curry, while Lanie opted for a burger with a side salad. The food arrived quickly, and as they ate, Lanie gave in to her curiosity, asking Jordan any question that popped into her mind.

She found out about Jordan's long-distance studies and the challenges he'd faced while working and studying at the same time. She learned more about the roles Bart Graw and Roger Greenwich, the former head of the organization now led by Jane Graw, had played in his life, both men serving as father figures when he'd sought advice on topics he hadn't wanted to bring to his mother. She also learned a lot more about the Graw siblings who owned the resort and seemed to be like brothers to Jordan.

"So, you're glad you have your best friend home, but you now have to share him with Jane?" she asked, deciding she might as well be nosy as long as Jordan kept answering her questions.

Clearly not in the least bothered by her question, Jordan just laughed. "I guess you could say that, though I'm happy he found her. It's nice to know he's so happy and settled down now. If it were me, I wouldn't want to go back to bachelor life either." He laughed good-naturedly.

Having cleaned his kitchen on more than one occasion, Lanie knew his fridge looked like that of a stereotypical bachelor. His staples were deli meat, milk for his cereal, and random assortments of chocolate bars and fruits.

"Don't tell me you don't enjoy being single." As a good-looking guy working in a luxury resort, she doubted he had any trouble meeting someone if he didn't want to be single.

"Well, since I shouldn't date employees" —he gave her a pointed look, his eyes sparkling with mischief— "and I don't date resort guests as a rule, it's actually harder than you might think to meet someone."

"And so you have to make do with me today." She couldn't help her satisfied expression. She'd tried for weeks to avoid him as best as she could, but something about Jordan made her want to be brave and put herself out there. Maybe it was her first impression of him, her fairy-tale prince, but more likely, it was his persistently open and kind attitude toward her.

Only right now, his eyes conveyed more than friendliness. He was looking at her with an electric intensity, and her tongue darted out to wet her suddenly dry lips. His eyes narrowed in on her mouth, making the feeling she'd felt in her belly earlier hum in her core.

"How about we take some dessert to go?" he asked, his voice sounding huskier than before.

Lanie nodded, and Jordan waved their server over,

ordering a small selection of their raw cacao treats.

When Jordan insisted on paying, Lanie tried to refuse, but he gave her a brilliant smile, reminding her that he'd sprung this excursion on her, so the least he could do was treat her to lunch. Perhaps she would have argued more, but her meager income was just enough to pay her rent and food, and the money she'd taken with her when she'd left her old life was almost completely used up. So, she thanked him, and they strolled out of the restaurant and down a sandy path that led them to the beach.

They took off their sandals and walked down to the water, the hot sand massaging Lanie's feet. With the shallow waves pushing white foam around their ankles, they headed down the beach, Jordan carrying the bag with their desserts.

"Do you like it here?" he asked suddenly, and Lanie nodded automatically.

"It's beautiful. Honestly, I never imagined myself living somewhere as exotic as here, but now that I am, I'm falling more and more in love with the idea of making this my home."

Her answer rang true, and for a second, Lanie was surprised at the serenity of the feelings that accompanied her words. She might have rationally decided to make this her home, but this was the first time she realized that these

Caribbean islands had become a place she liked for more than the refuge they offered her. This wasn't just a temporary vacation paradise for her but was also a place that had somehow lodged itself in her heart.

A wide smile played around Jordan's lips, and he looked pleased. Before Lanie could think of changing the topic, he asked another question, and she knew they'd reached the point where Jordan's own curiosity was coming through. "What made you decide to apply at Howler Island?"

Relieved, she realized that this was a question she could answer honestly. "Actually, I didn't have much of a plan other than looking for a job. When I met Mama Lita, she just kind of swept me up and brought me to interview with you."

When Jordan's forehead wrinkled, Lanie quickly spoke again. "Of course, I like the job and am glad she did, but more importantly, when can we start with those desserts? The cacao smells delicious."

His expression showed that Jordan hadn't missed her intentional change in topic, but he seemed to decide that he'd just go with it. "There are a few hammocks over there. I thought that'd be a good spot. Do you see them?" He pointed to a couple of red- and white-striped hammocks not too far down the beach.

"Sounds perfect. I'll race you." With that, Lanie started down the beach, hearing Jordan's feet splash in the water after her.

Being chased by a man suddenly felt a whole lot more exciting.

CHAPTER 8

The way Lanie's pants hugged her hips was more than a little distracting.

Even though she was sprinting across the sand, Jordan was certain he could pass her, but then he'd miss out on the view. He already knew the spectacular shape of her legs—her work uniform showed them off—but today, on their day off, he didn't feel quite as guilty admiring Lanie as usual.

She was stunning. Her hips had the perfect roundness, though her legs looked slender. He could have sworn that she'd lost weight since arriving on Howler Island.

He'd caught her hesitation to answer earlier, but given that he'd more or less tricked her into this date today, it was only fair that she wasn't willing to put herself out there completely, especially since she was already so much more open than she was at work. Today, she smiled easily and hadn't hesitated before agreeing to be in his company. When she'd taken his arm this morning, he'd been equally pleased and surprised.

She wasn't different from yesterday evening, though.

The Lanie he was with today was the type of woman who had the passion in her to give in to the brewing chemistry between them, a woman who was romantic enough to believe in a connection worthy of a kiss.

Before, her reserved beauty had intrigued him, but today she mesmerized him with a brilliant charm that wasn't comparable to anything he'd ever experienced. The way she looked at him was different somehow, less worried and filled with an interest that encouraged his own optimism.

Once they'd each claimed a hammock and spread the treats out between them, they reached down simultaneously to pick up the first dessert. Lanie's giggle told him she was perfectly at ease with him right now, and the knowledge pleased him more then he'd admit.

He watched as she nibbled a piece of the smooth, round cacao ball.

"Oh, my lord, these are delicious! What are they?"

"They've got dates, walnuts, and raw cacao in them. Probably some other stuff, but the sweetness comes from the dates." Was there something more erotic than watching a woman lick chocolate off her lips? Jordan shifted in his hammock and intentionally moved his eyes higher until he saw the delight in Lanie's eyes.

Yes, this had been a great plan.

"They're perfect."

He still hadn't taken a bite of his own treat, too mesmerized by the way Lanie's lips closed around the food, her eyes shut in enjoyment. She truly was even more beautiful right now than he'd ever seen her. He was sure of that. He'd suspected that she had this energy in her, a spark of her inner strength coming through when she didn't pay attention, but he'd never dreamed of seeing her so fully relaxed.

The first few weeks she'd been around the resort, she'd been as skittish as a young caiman. So what if she didn't want to share everything about her past? He truly didn't need to know. What he was much more interested in was her future. And this very moment.

He brought his own dessert to his mouth, allowing the mix of bitter chocolate, earthy walnuts, and sweet dates to relax him into the experience he wanted Lanie to have. Because showing her how amazing it was here, how much this area had to offer her, was suddenly very high on his list of priorities.

148

The next thing they tried were the raw cacao peanut butter cups. They'd already started to soften, and Jordan watched as Lanie licked the melted chocolate off her fingers after she ate the cup in one bite. He couldn't quite decide if buying these treats was the best thing he'd ever done in his life or the purest form of torture. He was starting to revert into a horny teenager, but he couldn't help himself.

Nothing could have prepared him for the sensual image of a perfectly content Lanie letting her tongue catch every last speck of chocolate. That they were completely alone on this stretch of beach didn't escape him, either.

Suddenly, he regretted the suggestion to come to the hammocks where their bodies were a meter apart, stuck in their respective lounging positions. It felt more like being strapped in a giant chastity belt than lying in probably the most beautiful spot in the world.

"I think I'll have to come here every day off that I have from now on," Lanie declared with conviction, and Jordan had to grin at her, something he found himself doing a lot.

Perhaps the hammocks were a blessing in disguise. Lanie wasn't someone he wanted to rush things with. More and more, it felt like she was worth being patient for.

"Just make sure you let me tag along."

Her eyes met his, and suddenly, her expression grew

more serious. "I think I'd like that." The words were exactly what he wanted to hear, but her tone suggested that she was unsure how she felt about them.

He'd simply have to prove how good of an idea it was. "How about we eat the brownies now?" It was the last dessert he'd ordered for them, knowing that the rich chocolaty flavor could get overwhelming if overindulged. The brownies were his favorite, though, and they would definitely work in his favor.

"You don't have to ask me twice."

Lanie finished her brownie first, and Jordan suggested that they walk one of the jungle trails that he knew would bring them past a small waterfall. It was well into the afternoon now, but he didn't want the day to end just yet. As much as he enjoyed Lanie's company and wanted to respect her boundaries, he also wanted to learn at least a little more about her.

"How do you find it, living with roommates?" The question seemed to be a safe one since he was basing it on information he already knew about her, and sure enough, Lanie began talking without the telltale pause that always came when she avoided sharing something.

"I'm surprised how easy it's been. Honestly, it reminds me of my university days. Gabriela could easily be one of the girls who used to be in my dorm." Lanie laughed, and Jordan suppressed his surprise, not wanting to make her regret that she'd shared something about her past, after all. She'd gone to college.

He already knew she spoke two languages, and based on her manner of speaking, it was clear that she was intelligent, but he had assumed that perhaps she'd received a less conventional education. Maybe that she'd lived in different countries, picking Spanish up that way.

Why else would someone choose to work in a housekeeping position that required no educational qualifications? There was nothing wrong with the job, but she could easily get something that paid better, and it made him wonder what had brought her here. He knew better than to ask, though, so he simply glanced over at her with a smile to encourage her to continue talking.

"Mama Lita could easily qualify as the RA." Again, Lanie was laughing, but this time, Jordan interrupted her.

"What's an RA?"

Lanie looked at him with surprise. "A resident advisor. You know, the students who live in the dorms? They're responsible for keeping everyone in order. Don't you have them here?"

"I did long-distance courses and never lived on

campus, remember? I wouldn't be able to tell you." He could tell the exact moment she realized that she'd inadvertently told him she held a degree that she'd neglected to mention when she'd applied for her job. Maybe she'd dropped out before finishing, though. But before he could ask her, Lanie had already reverted to their previous topic.

"Eventually, I think I'd like to rent one of the available apartments above the bars. I know the noise is probably bad, but I'd be able to afford one by myself and I'd have an amazing view out onto the water and the surrounding islands."

Her words served as an effective distraction. "So, you're really going to stay here then?"

Lanie's smile moved back up to her eyes. "The company around here is pretty decent, so yes, this will be my home. You know, unless my terrible boss fires me."

Now it was his turn to laugh. "I think you're safe there."

The rest of the hike was spent talking about the foods they liked, movies and shows they enjoyed, and books they'd read. Lanie was well-read and had a disconcerting obsession with epic fantasies. While Jordan enjoyed watching *The Lord of The Rings*, the idea of ever having to read J. R. R. Tolkien again was enough to make him want to run for the hills. There just weren't enough hours in the day for so many pointless countryside descriptions when one could simply enjoy the beauty of New Zealand on the screen. But that hardly mattered because the hike was more fun than Jordan could have ever hoped for, and they easily continued their banter about popular culture as they took the boat back to Bocas.

Before Lanie could climb out of the boat, Jordan reached out to place his hand on hers. He'd tied the boat to a small public dock that was bordered on each side by covered private decks, giving them some privacy. The urge to keep their day together going was strong, but Jordan knew that it wasn't a good idea for him to walk Lanie home, where Gabriela and Mama Lita would be waiting for her.

He was left with only one option if he wanted more time with her, so he allowed his lips to spread into the grin he knew made him look mischievous. The same grin had often helped him get out of trouble with his mother when he'd still been a boy. "I had a great time today, Lanie. Thank you for letting me take you."

"I had fun, too." The sparkle in her eyes told him she was telling the truth, and the knowledge encouraged him to press forward.

"Now that we're agreed that I didn't pressure you

yesterday and you've tasted some of what I've got to offer, maybe you'll agree to another date with me?"

The way Lanie's lips broke into a grin told him she hadn't missed his innuendo, but her response still surprised him.

"So, it really was a date." Lanie laughed. Then she pushed a strand of hair back before she lifted her eyes back to his. "I would like that."

Excitement rushed through him. "If I didn't make it apparent that today turned into a date by now, perhaps this will convince you."

Like last time, he leaned forward slowly, giving Lanie time to decide, but she didn't need any. Her lips met his, and he could still taste the sweetness of the dates they'd eaten earlier on her lips. More than any dessert, he couldn't get enough of her taste, and for a glorious minute he indulged in a sweet kiss. Before he got swept up in the endorphins and testosterone flooding his body, he pulled back.

He wasn't interested in a fling. Lanie wasn't a woman he wanted to rush anything with. This kiss was only a promise for more, and he hoped more than anything that she'd take him up on the offer.

* * *

Lanie felt lighter than she had in over a year. The day had been amazing. Over the past months, she'd slowly begun to relax, but until today, she hadn't quite managed to feel like her old self, always carrying the weight of the lingering paranoia that Collin would somehow find her or that she'd get a call from her parents that he'd started to harass them.

Today had been a turning point, she was sure of that. There had been a few moments during their little trip today when her past had thrown a shadow over the day, but those moments had been insignificant. Somehow, Jordan's presence had allowed her to move on quickly without sinking back into the tight restraints of the constant worry that had started back when Mona had first started dating her new boyfriend. Even before Mona had confided her own worries to Lanie, something about Collin had felt off.

Two years of worries and stress, but here she was, starting a new life and just maybe something more, something with Jordan that she hadn't even dreamed of being a possibility before.

When Collin's trial had been going on, she'd asked herself why she hadn't trusted her instincts sooner, and for a long while, she hadn't been sure she'd ever be able to trust another man again. The risk that she might miss something about them was too great, but now she knew she'd been wrong. She was stronger than that and she could still find her way back to the person she used to be. Someone who believed in true love and soulmates.

They had avoided any serious conversations aside from Jordan's revelation that he'd made his boss aware of their kiss. Lanie almost had to giggle as she thought about his serious expression when they'd sat in the restaurant. Could there be a more obvious sign that Jordan was a good guy?

The walk from the pier to the rundown house, just past the grocer who placed his produce display well into the street, went by in less time than it did other days, and Lanie stepped into the cool air of her current home. She hadn't truly thought through her next steps, but when she told Jordan today that she was going to look into finding an apartment, it had ignited a spark of determination.

She liked living with Gabriela and Mama Lita, but she'd always liked having her own space, and now that she'd set her mind to moving on, not just physically but emotionally as well, she couldn't stay with roommates. It was a crutch. Something to make her feel safe when she still remembered what it was like to have someone break into your private refuge and scare you enough to make you move to a different country and start a new life from scratch.

Collin wouldn't find her here, and she needed to stop worrying that someone else, someone like Jordan, would uncover that she was using a fake name. Even if someone were to figure it out, that still didn't mean that Collin would automatically learn of her whereabouts. No, it was time to move on and truly look toward her future.

With a swing in her steps, she entered the house, finding it empty. Going upstairs, Lanie undressed in her room, ready to wash off the sand that clung to her from their day at the beach. Stepping into the shower, she turned the water to a medium heat. Before coming to the south, she'd always enjoyed her showers hot, but here, adding more heat to the day simply didn't feel right. Instead, the warm water provided the perfect mix of comfort and refreshment, and Lanie closed her eyes as she dipped her head back, enjoying the way the water added weight to her hair.

Once her thick hair was finally soaked through, she reached up to grab her shampoo and found the ledge that usually held all her products missing the big bottle that held the affordable shampoo she'd bought at the local store. It was gone.

Her muscles tensed as terror washed over her.

She still remembered Mona coming to her,

complaining of little items being misplaced in her house after she'd finally left Collin. They hadn't made the connection then, even laughing about Mona's scatterbrained mind, but eventually, Mona hadn't laughed anymore.

Eventually, they'd both accepted that those missing things that had seemed so insignificant at the time had been the first warning signs that Collin wouldn't allow Mona to just walk away. That he'd developed an obsession. Despite the lengthy court hearings after Collin had escalated to physical violence, his obsession hadn't faded away. He had only become angrier.

Eventually, Mona had given up hope.

Lanie would never forget Mona's face the day she'd left. Her best friend had cried so much in the prior months, but that day, Mona hadn't shed a tear as she'd met Lanie in the park where they'd played together as kids. She'd simply told Lanie that she was leaving.

Collin's year-long sentence for sexual assault had begun a month earlier, and Lanie had been hopeful that perhaps Mona could finally move past the horror of having a stalker. She'd known that her friend would carry the scars from that final attack with her for life and had been determined to be as supportive as she could possibly be, but at least now,

Collin was where he belonged.

All the while, Mona had known better. She'd known that it wasn't the end. It was simply a minute interruption from Collin's constant threats. Mona and her parents had left without leaving a number or address to reach them. Instead, her friend had hugged her fiercely and had told Lanie she was sorry.

Even the memory of that moment still evoked the same feeling of devastation she'd felt then. She'd even been mad. Mad at Mona for leaving. Mad at Mona's parents for helping her make that decision, and most of all, mad at Collin for taking her best friend away from her. But later, she'd come to understand. When Collin was released early and had started to walk past Lanie's house every day, she'd finally understood.

There was no escaping an obsession like Collin's, and when Mona wasn't there to target anymore, Lanie had become his next victim, terrified to leave her house. He blamed her for taking Mona away from him, even though she'd been mourning the loss of her best friend herself.

When she'd realized that things had started to go missing from her own house, she'd turned to her parents. Her father had new papers for her within two weeks, while her mother hadn't let her go out of her sights for even ten minutes. The memory of Mona's beaten and abused body in the hospital had still been too fresh.

Finally, Lanie had boarded a plane. Using her real passport, she'd bought a last-minute ticket right at the airport, not bothering to listen to where she was flying. She'd done this twice more, choosing connecting flights at random. Once she'd landed here, she no longer went by Lori, using the name on the fake paperwork instead.

Lanie had been what her grandmother used to call her, and it felt comforting to know that she still had that tie to her family. She'd never gone by her full name, Lorraine, and responding to Lanie had come easily. There was no way Collin could know about the pet name her grandmother had used for her when she was a kid, but her father had rightfully assumed it would be easier for her to have a name that felt familiar.

Luckily, while she hadn't dared to use the forgeries for international travel, they'd held up for the employment paperwork.

Now, she was tempted to pack her bags and leave as fast as she could. Once she'd managed to dry herself off, hands shaking, she walked into her bedroom. Before she could even reach under the bed for her luggage, she heard voices downstairs.

160

Female voices, Lanie realized as her breath left her body in a whoosh.

Gabriela and Mama Lita were home, and even though the panic was still there, Lanie managed to put on her clothes and walk downstairs. She wasn't alone in the house. What had seemed like a crutch earlier was now the only thing that kept her from racing to the airport.

"Hey, you, where did you disappear to today?" Gabriela asked in a chipper tone.

For a moment, Lanie couldn't even recall where she'd been, but then Jordan's face popped into her mind. The thought of him made her breath catch. She'd never find out whether there could have been more between them if she left now.

"Uhm, I went to this restaurant where they serve all these raw cacao desserts."

Mama Lita nodded. "That would be the Cocoa Playa."

"Oh, it's good, isn't it?" Gabriela asked, still enthusiastic.

Meanwhile, Mama Lita's eyes had caught Lanie's expression. She couldn't be sure what the older woman saw, but Lanie assumed it must be some version of the shock she was still under. Whatever it was, Mama Lita came over and took her hand.

161

"You're freezing. Are you getting sick?"

"Uhm, no. It's just . . . my shampoo was missing." She knew she probably wasn't making much sense, but she just couldn't figure out what else to say.

"Oh, shoot. I meant to leave you a note, but I forgot." Gabriela was speaking, but Lanie was only listening with one ear.

Should she give Mama Lita a note for Jordan when she left, or should she go to the resort herself and tell him she was moving away?

"Here." Mama Lita stepped away as Gabriela held something out for Lanie to take. Confused, she accepted the plastic bottle and stared at it for a moment before realizing she was holding the same shampoo that had gone missing from her bathroom, except this bottle was completely full.

"Yeah, sorry I just took yours, but I was all out, and I figured I was going shopping anyway so I could replace it right away. I didn't realize you'd be home and showering before I could bring you the new bottle."

The shaking should have stopped at Gabriela's words. Relief should be flooding her veins, but all Lanie could manage was a forced smile and a nod. Then, she fled back into her bedroom, tears streaming down her cheeks.

CHAPTER 9

All day, Jordan had kept an eye out for Lanie. He'd hoped to catch sight of her, not even sure what he'd do if he actually ran into her. He couldn't just disrupt her during her work hours, but he still wanted to speak with her and ask what her plans were for her next day off, but until now, he hadn't seen her.

All morning, he'd suppressed the urge, but as his lunch break approached, he gave in and opened the cleaning schedule on his computer. Lanie had her lunch break right now, which meant she was probably in the break room. It wouldn't do to just show up and ask her to come outside, so he quickly looked up Gabriela's schedule.

On the way to the welcome center, he gave in to an internal monologue about the absurdity of how he was acting, but he wasn't having much luck convincing himself that he should back off and wait until they could see each other somewhere other than at the resort. Lanie was the first woman on the island who'd tempted him to break his dating rules, and if Saturday had told him anything, it was that she was worth taking a risk for.

He was ready for more than a fling, and she needed to know that he was serious about getting to know her.

"Dude, I've been trying to catch your attention for a full minute. What are you daydreaming about?" Logan's mocking voice startled Jordan enough that he almost ran into Logan's golf cart when he turned around. He hadn't even heard his friend drive up behind him, which was now giving Logan enough ammunition to bend over laughing.

When Logan finally calmed down, Jordan gave him his best mock scowl. "I liked you better when you were a brooding teenager. This happy version of you is getting on my nerves." Perhaps Logan would have taken him seriously if Jordan had managed to keep the scowl in place, which he hadn't.

"Are you headed to the welcome center?" Logan asked, ignoring Jordan's comment entirely.

"Ah, yes, actually."

Raising his eyebrows, Logan grinned again. "Don't tell me you're now stalking the employees. Or rather, a specific employee."

That had been exactly what he'd been planning to do, but he quickly shook his head. "Don't be an idiot. I was on my way to chat with Gabriela. She's helping organize the midsummer party this year."

Logan's face lit up. "Oh, yes, that'll be fun. Jump in. I'm on my way to the center myself. I chatted with my HR department to come up with a solution for your little dating problem." Again, Logan could barely contain his smug grin, and Jordan satisfied his annoyance with a punch against Logan's shoulder as he climbed into the golf cart.

He should have known better than to expect that Logan would let him get away with his infatuation with Lanie without at least the minimum of teasing. Being with your childhood friends almost guaranteed that you reverted to teenage idiocy whenever an opportunity arose, and given that he felt like a crushing teenager half the time he was around Lanie, it only seemed fitting.

"What did you and HR cook up for us?" Jordan asked before they reached the welcome center.

"Actually, it seemed a good idea to have a designated position for these types of concerns, so instead of simply going up to your manager or boss, we now have someone from HR in headquarters who will serve as a contact point for everyone from any of my resorts who would like to disclose a relationship or discuss any concerns."

Jordan nodded, satisfied that this would ensure there wouldn't be anything overlooked now that he'd taken the first steps of courting Lanie.

When they arrived, they ignored the construction still ongoing in the main offices and headed over to the marina office. Logan had several printouts with the contact information of the HR representative and walked purposefully into the office that currently served as the temporary break room.

When they entered, the room quieted and heads swiveled in their direction. Jordan could feel his mouth turn into an involuntary grin. Apparently, they'd made quite the entrance.

"Hello, ladies and gentlemen," Logan greeted with his typical formality, though he smiled at his employees like they were old friends. "I'm just here to make a quick announcement and hang up a flyer before I let Jordan here talk to you about the upcoming party."

He was met with curious stares, but Jordan was too busy looking for Lanie to properly listen to what Logan was saying. She was standing in the back, giving him a reserved smile before focusing on what Logan was explaining.

166

Her eyes widened as she listened to Logan talk about the new liaison for anything relationship and sexual harassment related before they flew back to Jordan. Obviously, she knew what had initiated these changes, and Jordan could just make out the faint blush that colored her cheeks. His own smile grew. She really was gorgeous. But before he could enjoy the moment any longer, her expression shifted to one of worry.

It was the same strained expression he'd seen a lot on her before Saturday. He'd hoped that their little excursion to Cacao Playa was enough to put her at ease, but it was obvious that there was still something on her mind now that they were back at the resort.

He'd have to speak with her privately and make sure that Logan's announcement hadn't upset her. Perhaps she thought he was trying to cover himself from potential backlash when really, what he wanted was to make sure she felt secure in her employment, no matter whether she decided to give him a shot or not. And he darn well hoped she'd go out with him again.

"Okay, people, that's all I had, so now I'll let Jordan talk to you about the midsummer party."

Jordan quickly tore his eyes away from Lanie to scan the room. There were about twelve people here, and fortunately, Gabriela was indeed one of them. Since Logan had picked him up on the way, he hadn't had any time to plan what he wanted to say, so he'd have to wing it.

"As you know, we have a midsummer party each year, an evening when we usually do a big barbecue to show our appreciation for all the good work you do for us year-round. This year, Gabriela has stepped up to take the lead and figure out what we need for this year's party. Like last year, we'll have live music, which I've already booked. We'll also have some sort of food selection, drinks, and perhaps some other entertainment going on. I wanted to come up here and get everyone to start thinking about it. Gabriela, if you're still up for it, perhaps you can collect the ideas over the next week, and then we'll start putting down numbers. Everyone can bring their families, just like always. I'll just need a rough idea of how many people will be there so I can get the orders right."

"I'll bring you a list with what we have in mind by next week," Gabriela said, beaming with enthusiasm. The rest of the people in the room hummed with happy agreement.

When Jordan's eyes drifted back to Lanie, he found her stiffly standing near the back wall giving him a forced looking smile. It was like a déjà vu. How could she look at him almost exactly like she had in the first few weeks on the island when just yesterday, they'd shared a kiss goodbye?

He really needed to speak with her and figure out what was making her retreat when everything inside him screamed full speed ahead. Unfortunately, he couldn't think of a good excuse to call her out with him, so he shot her one last look and then left the room after calling a goodbye to everyone.

Well, that had been a failure, but he wouldn't let that discourage him just yet.

* * *

By the end of Lanie's shift, Jordan had a plan. He had his boat ready at the pier that they usually used for the shuttle boat, which would arrive in thirty minutes to take the day shift back to Glamirante or Bocas, wherever people needed to go. When he spotted Gabriela, he waved at her.

"Hey, do you want a lift? I'm headed into town."

"Yes, sure, thank you," she called and quickly grabbed her stuff.

Jordan waited for her to approach him before he asked, "Is Lanie going back too? Should we wait for her?"

An amused smile spread across Gabriela's face, and Jordan got the distinct impression that everyone was making fun of him today. "She should be out any minute now. Have you guys properly met yet?"

"Of course we have. Last week, she did the cleaning at my place, actually."

"Ah, no better way to get to know someone than by scrubbing their bathroom." Gabriela laughed. Instead of sarcasm, her laughter was full of actual humor, and Jordan couldn't help but join in.

"As you can see, I'm in desperate need of a more suitable environment to get to know our newest team member." He tried to play it cool, though Gabriela's raised eyebrows told him he was failing miserably.

"Desperate, huh? Well, perhaps you should come to our place for dinner then?"

"That'd be great." This was working out even better than he'd hoped.

A smug smile stretched over Gabriela's face. "You know, unless it interferes with the business you have to do in Bocas?"

When he gave her a confused look, Gabriela added, "You know, the reason you're taking your boat over right now and are conveniently able to give us a lift?"

"Oh, that. Yes, I can do that right quick."

Just then, Lanie came walking toward them and

Gabriela waved her over. "Jordan here has offered to give us a ride over."

When Lanie blushed slightly, Gabriela burst into laughter. "Well, that explains Logan's spiel about fraternization today."

Finally, Lanie's face changed into her beautiful smile and she winked at him. "It seems our manager likes to do things the right way."

Ignoring Gabriela, Jordan grinned at Lanie. "I'm an all-in kind of guy."

When they arrived at Mama Lita's house, pots and pans were already banging in the kitchen, saving him from Mama Lita's lecture on not coming to visit often enough. Gabriela ushered him and Lanie to sit in the living room. With a wink, she excused herself to help Mama Lita with the food.

Lanie was smiling at him now, her expression amused. "So, your boss doesn't sit on his hands, does he?"

Relieved to find she hadn't retreated into her reserved shell again, he grinned. "No, Logan doesn't do slow. He's always fully invested in his businesses, and he likes to get stuff done right away."

"Which is probably why he's so successful."

Jordan nodded. Lanie was right. Even if Logan often

insisted that he could never have achieved what he did without Jordan's financial backing, Jordan knew the opposite was true. Logan had always been driven and smart. He would have been successful even without the money Jordan's mother had saved up.

Lanie looked thoughtful. "But he's also philanthropic according to what I found online. I searched Graw Resorts on the break room computer when you first hired me, and I read a bit about the nature reserves and animal rescues his resorts fund. It's an interesting marketing strategy they're using. In fact, I wouldn't be surprised if they could successfully expand the reach of their initiatives if they integrated the same principles they use for their non-profit slogans in their resort ads."

Lanie stood up from the couch she'd been sitting on and paced the room. "Imagine this—wealthy clients looking for a luxury vacation but also an opportunity to post about themselves on social media. If the resort, besides being eco-friendly, which is already good, provided an opportunity for clients to emphasize that their stay isn't only non-damaging to the environment but actually improving it by helping to protect endangered species, then their clients could portray themselves as doing the planet a favor by going on their extravagant trip."

Lanie's excited smile beamed down at him. "Right now, Graw resorts is already using its resorts to help fund the non-profits indirectly, but they could actually drive clients to their resorts by using the non-profits as a selling point, turning it into a win-win situation."

* * *

Jordan stared at her, and it took Lanie a moment to realize that she'd gotten carried away with her enthusiasm.

She'd already let slip that she'd gone to college. If he now realized she had a degree and several years of work experience in marketing, he'd start asking questions she wasn't prepared to answer. Luckily, Mama Lita called that dinner was ready in that moment, and they both headed into the kitchen, allowing Lanie to escape with only a curious look from Jordan.

The comfortable way Jordan fit into their group of women didn't surprise Lanie. He was the type of person who was easily liked, and she found herself watching him joke with Gabriela and Mama Lita, torn between longing and uncertainty.

Dipping some bread into the tomato soup, Lanie was sure of one thing. Falling for Jordan would be so easy if only she could bring herself to stop second-guessing her choice to make Howler Island her home.

Yesterday, she'd been certain, but today, she kept thinking how Mona had never meant for Lanie's life to be uprooted because of Collin. And yet, here she was, away from where she'd grown up, unable to work in the career she'd loved, and panicking about little things like a missing shampoo bottle.

What if Collin found her after all, and then someone else would suffer the consequences? What if he came here and decided to stalk Mama Lita or Gabriela next? Or maybe even Jordan?

"What's going on with you, girl?" Gabriela interrupted her thoughts, and Lanie realized she'd simply been staring at Jordan, not paying attention to the conversation going on around her.

"Ah, nothing, sorry. What were you saying?"

"I was asking whether you wanted to help set up for the midsummer party. It's in two weeks, and I'm starting to poll everyone."

"Oh, yes, of course." Now that she knew Collin hadn't broken into her bathroom, she could stay and help her friend. She'd overreacted yesterday and was still letting her thoughts run wild. One stupid missing shampoo bottle had thrown her back into the paranoia she'd worked so hard to overcome. Perhaps, if she managed to overcome her latest shock, she didn't need to leave. She could stay and spend more time with Jordan.

When she raised her eyes to look at him across the table, he was already studying her, and she had to smile. What was it about him that made her feel so much lighter, less anxious, and more eager for her future?

It was as if he'd sensed her worries earlier at work and had gone out of his way to spend the evening together, lending her his happiness and helping her realize that she was okay and that nothing had changed about her plans to make Howler Island her home.

After they finished dinner, Jordan announced that he had to run an errand, asking if anyone else needed to walk into town. Lanie didn't need anything, but she readily agreed to walk with him, much to Gabriela's amusement. Clearly, they weren't being very subtle, and Lanie grinned at Jordan as they stepped onto the sidewalk.

"I don't think they suspect a thing," she stage-whispered. His answering laugh made butterflies appear in her stomach. It was a feeling she hadn't had since her very first big crush in high school, something she'd always associated with a childish kind of infatuation.

When Jordan and she had kissed that very first time, she'd felt passion awaken in her, and Saturday after their trip, she'd felt longing and excitement at his kiss, but these butterflies were new. Like spring, when the beautiful creatures used to appear out in her parents' back yard, this feeling told her something beautiful was happening. She impulsively took Jordan's hand.

Surprised, he looked down before giving her a wicked grin. "No, I think we've been very sneaky." Then he leaned forward and kissed her gently on the lips.

Like the last kiss, he kept the contact feather light, but inside her the butterfly wings flapped fiercely, and Lanie leaned in closer, eager to taste more of him.

Behind them, the door opened, and Gabriela chuckled. "Well, look at that. Nicely done, Lanie."

Lanie looked at her friend who held up the organic compost.

"I'm just bringing this out. Didn't expect to still find you two out here."

Something about the way she said it told Lanie that Gabriela wasn't exactly telling the truth. Her eyes shifted over to the window where Mama Lita stood watching them with a satisfied smirk.

"Right," Jordan answered, clearly coming to the same

conclusion as Lanie. "Well, we'd better run that important errand now."

When he took her hand and pulled her toward the sidewalk with a low chuckle, Lanie threw a glance over her shoulder and winked at Mama Lita.

* * *

As they walked down the narrow road, Jordan could feel that Lanie was studying him.

He was glad he'd decided to come here tonight, but Lanie's behavior was a puzzle to him. Her comments about Graw Resorts earlier confirmed that she was overqualified for the position she currently held, and yet she'd seemed upset to have slipped and given him a glimpse at what she might be like if she didn't guard herself so closely.

Why was she selling herself short?

She wouldn't be the only one around here who took a job because of necessity, rather than passion or qualification, but most people he knew would do a lot to climb the ladder and improve their economic position. Lanie was doing the opposite.

She seemed happy enough to spend time with him, their hands interlocked as they headed toward Main Street, but she still didn't seem to trust him. As much as he liked spending time with her, they would need to talk soon. If his biological father had taught him one thing, it was that heartbreak followed when one person kept parts of their life secret from the other. His father had never intended to stay with his mother, not even when she'd been pregnant.

What was Lanie keeping from him?

She'd changed into a pair of cut off jeans and a simple red shirt. Her dark hair hung loose over her tanned shoulders, and she didn't wear a speck of makeup. When he smiled at her, her lips curved up in response. Her eyes crinkled at the corners, and he almost gave in and kissed her again, but he held back instead.

They reached the intersection, and he motioned for them to walk toward the side that held fewer tourist shops.

"You've never told me what made you want to travel," Lanie prompted after they'd walked in silence for a little while.

It was nice that she was interested in his life, even if half the time it felt like she was trying to distract him from asking her any questions in turn. It might be conceited, but it was flattering that as interested as he was in her, she at least seemed to return his curiosity. And his kisses.

He doubted that Lanie was hiding another family

elsewhere, the way his father had hidden his wife and children from Jordan's mother during their brief affair, but it was obvious that she was hiding something, and as long as he couldn't be sure that said something wouldn't affect him too, he couldn't risk falling for her. Falling for her more than he already had, anyway.

He gently pressed her hand, hoping to show that he appreciated her efforts to get to know each other better. "I was raised by my mother on Howler Island. My father was someone who vacationed there for a while, and they had an affair. He left, and I never met him, but when he died, I was notified. I'm not sure why, but it made me want to figure out if I was missing out on something by never leaving."

"And you realized you've got everything you want here?" The intensity with which Lanie asked the question surprised him. Somehow, more rode on his answer than he could possibly understand, but instead of sharing where her question was coming from, Lanie had once again directed the conversation away from herself.

It was time to be direct and figure out where he stood. "I don't have everything I want just yet. I see Logan and Jane, who're happy together and settled down, and it's something I want someday, too. But until now, I haven't met the right woman yet." He reached out and took Lanie's hand. "It's important to me that I find someone who loves this place as much as I do. Someone who is sure they want to call Howler Island their home and not leave when they're over their stint in paradise, ready to return to some big city."

At his words, Lanie flinched slightly, and Jordan could feel his stomach drop. She'd told him she was looking to make this her home, had even considered where she wanted to live, so what about his statement made her react like that?

It was possible that he was moving too fast, but he felt ready to be serious with someone, and he liked Lanie. He liked her smile and her enthusiasm when she wasn't caught up in whatever had her so worried and anxious all the time. What was the point in pretending to want something casual when it would just waste their time if she wasn't looking for the same thing?

"You're not interested in settling down permanently? Maybe even get married someday?" he asked, trying and failing to keep his tone casual. They were still strolling down Main Street, and he had no specific place in mind that he wanted to go since his errand had been nothing but a ruse to see Lanie.

Lanie hesitated with her answer, and it was just long enough to let him doubt her when she finally spoke. "No, I do. It's not that."

She stopped walking and turned to looked at him as if she knew that her answer mattered to him more than he wanted to let on. "I'd love to call this home and find someone to spend my life with. My parents have a very happy marriage, and I want the same thing for myself. Until now, I just never met the right person, I guess." She looked up at him almost shyly, and hope sparked in him again.

Looking down at their hands still intertwined between them, Jordan suddenly hated the uncertainty. What would it be like if she rejected him now? Part of him realized that he barely knew Lanie, but something else told him that the way her hand fit perfectly into his meant something. They just worked together.

She was smart and interesting, beyond the mystery of her aversion to sharing her past with him. When she let herself, she radiated the same love for life that he embraced. Maybe he didn't know her for a long time, but he knew she was worth taking a chance on, and so he asked the question that he suspected might push past what she was comfortable with. "So, you're interested in something more serious?"

It wasn't a great place or time to have this discussion, but he had to know. Everything she said sounded perfect, but her expression was subdued again. It was killing him to know what was going on in her head.

As he watched, Lanie's expression turned conflicted rather than excited, and warning bells went off where before there had still been hope.

The realization that he'd been wrong almost knocked the air out of him.

She wasn't ready to commit to staying here, wasn't ready to commit to more than a single date at a time.

If she wasn't willing to share why she'd moved here in the first place, if he never learned what was in her past that kept her so closed off, he'd never be sure she was here to stay. Even if everything else about her told him she was worth taking a chance on, this was a risk he couldn't take.

His mother's story had taught him the heartbreak that came with falling in love with someone who was intent on leaving you behind, and he'd sworn not to repeat her mistake.

CHAPTER 10

Jordan's question hung in the air between them.

He wanted her to decide whether she was ready for something serious between them, wanted to know whether she could move past her own fears. They'd both stopped on the near-empty sidewalk, and she looked into his eyes, wanting the lightness back that he usually seemed to emanate. But his eyes were serious now.

There was no way she could lie to him, no way that she'd abuse the trust he was extending to her. It was the reason she hadn't wanted to get close to anyone here, and now she needed to answer him because avoiding his question wasn't an option anymore. Not when he looked at her expectantly.

"Jordan, I want to be able to say yes, but there are some things in my life that are unpredictable, and as much as I want to settle down here—I really do—I'm not sure it would be fair to tell you I'm ready for something serious when that might pull you into my mess. In all truth, I might have to leave on short notice if something happens, and I don't want to leave you behind dealing with the consequences." Because she knew how awful that was. She looked into his eyes, willing him to understand how much she wanted what he was offering.

If they were to become serious, she couldn't guarantee that Collin wouldn't go after him. Collin had targeted her for the simple reason that she'd been Mona's best friend. Even when his obsession had been focused on Mona, he'd lashed out at Lanie for taking up too much of Mona's time, for poisoning Mona against him. He hadn't seen that he'd turned Mona against him all by himself. Rational explanations hadn't worked on Collin.

As she tried reading Jordan's expression, she knew she couldn't keep lying to him. As much as she'd tried to be honest, he still only knew her fake last name. At least her new first name didn't feel like a lie. Lanie was who she was now, and she'd gladly continue using the name if she had the chance to stay on Howler Island. Her grandmother would have liked that.

Perhaps he'd understand that she had a good reason

for pretending to be someone else, but it wouldn't change the fact that he'd have to report the false paperwork she'd used to his boss, and then he might get in trouble for her deceit. Or she'd ask him to keep her secret, placing him in a terrible position. She couldn't do that to him, not when she knew how much living here and being a member of the community meant to him. She couldn't ask him to jeopardize his values and friendship to Logan by asking him to lie for her.

"Can we talk about this at my place?" he asked, obviously realizing that the sidewalk in the late evening wasn't a suitable spot to have this conversation. His face had gone tight, but his tone remained gentle.

She nodded. Watching Jordan's expression stay carefully neutral, so different from his usual smiles, was painful to watch. The last thing she ever wanted to do was to take the happiness he always radiated away from him.

She would have loved to be the woman who could make him happy, the woman who deserved to be around him every day and watch him finally achieve the life he wanted. A life with a family to fill his home, a wife and children to explore the beaches and jungle with. Someone he could share the love he had for these islands with.

She followed Jordan to his boat, knowing that if she

didn't return to the house soon, Gabriela and Mama Lita would probably assume she'd gone home with Jordan. Only they would assume they were doing something completely different from talking. Something that in a different life, Lanie would have been more than happy to follow Jordan home for. Except, as she pictured the happiness Jordan deserved in his life, she also realized that she had no business leading him on. As much as she wanted the same thing, she couldn't even promise him that she was brave enough to stay here.

Her thoughts raced as Jordan sped across the water toward Howler Island.

What would happen the next time she misplaced an item or genuinely lost something? Would she be able to shake the panic and stick around, or would she run?

It was less than two years ago that Collin had escalated his stalking. His constant appearances had worn Mona down, just like the missing things she knew he'd taken, the little gifts he was leaving for her. The threats he'd made.

It had taken a long time to get enough evidence for a restraining order, but eventually, she'd succeeded, and Lanie had supported her as best as she could. Except that had meant she, too, had been harassed by Collin, and it had made her feel more vulnerable than she had ever let Mona know.

Her friend had needed Lanie's strength, so she'd kept her own fears to herself. Instead, she'd accompanied her bestie to all the legal appointments and had held Mona in her arms when her friend had sobbed after Collin had somehow gotten his hands on yet another new phone number. But then, one night, he'd gotten ahold of Mona when she'd left the bank, and Lanie hadn't been there to help her.

In the hospital, Mona hadn't been able to speak about the rape, but everyone had known. The subdued glances from the nurses, the sobbing of Mona's mother, the rage in her father's eyes. The only good thing that had come out of it had been Collin's arrest, but it could never make up for the pain Mona had to suffer. And when Collin couldn't locate Mona after they had released him, he'd focused on Lanie.

No, she wasn't sure she'd be brave enough to stay if she thought Collin were here.

She'd been brave for Mona, but her friend was gone now. Hopefully safe.

If Collin had found her, she didn't think she could stay. She'd want to go back home to her parents and family, go back to the place Collin had made her flee, because the only reason she'd given up her family had been the promise of safety. If that promise were gone, what would hold her here?

She watched Jordan tie his boat to the pier at Howler Island, and her heart told her the answer. Jordan was here.

But was that enough?

Jordan wanted to give them a shot, was willing to see if they might start their very own family someday. It was a wonderful thought, but they didn't really know each other well enough to be sure they would work well together. And even if everything inside her told her that Jordan was the man she could spend the rest of her life with and be happy, how could she ever justify pulling him into danger?

Even if nothing new happened, could she truthfully promise that she was planning to spend the rest of her life here if in the back of her mind, she kept an escape plan ready?

"Ready?" he asked, reaching his hand out to help her out of the boat. Lanie shook her head slightly but gave him a grateful smile.

"Thanks."

"Let's take a golf cart. As much as I enjoy going on walks, right now, I'd like to have some proper privacy so we can talk. You can trust me, you know?"

Lanie had to grin despite herself. With any other man, that question would have sounded borderline creepy. You can trust me—the tag line for every stalker turned serial killer. But Jordan she could trust, and the realization was painful and reassuring at the same time.

She made a decision then. Perhaps it was a selfish one, but with Jordan walking closely next to her, it still felt right. She'd warn him of the potential dangers and then see what he wanted to do. She'd give him the choice.

"I know, and I do trust you. I'll let you choose what you want to know, and I'll answer you honestly."

The corners of his mouth twitched upward slightly, but he didn't respond. Instead, he climbed into a golf cart, and when she slid onto the seat next to him, he took her hand. That she wanted to hold on to him for as long as she could made the drive to his villa much too short.

Inside the house, Jordan headed to his open kitchen area. "Can I get you something to drink?"

"Do you have some orange juice?" she asked, and Jordan nodded.

She sat down on the living room couch, watching him pour two glasses. It would have been nice to sit outside, but it was already growing dark outside, and trying to have a serious conversation while being eaten alive by mosquitoes seemed like a terrible combination.

When he sat down across from her, she took her glass from him and started her story without waiting for him to ask something. "There is a good reason for why I don't speak about who I was before I came here, and if you want me to tell you, you need to know that it might impact your job. It might even drag you into my mess."

"My job?" Jordan said, but he didn't sound as surprised as she would have expected. "If anything, you seem overqualified for the job I hired you for, and I've had no complaints about the work you're doing, so I'm guessing this is about why you came here, not what you're doing at the resort as part of your job. So why would that impact my job?"

"Because I haven't been honest about who I am, and if I tell you, you'll have to tell your boss, who is also your best friend, so you're pretty much double-obligated to share my story with him."

"And that would be so bad?"

It was the question that had been nagging at her, too. Would it truly be so bad?

Jordan would understand if she told him the entire story, and if she really thought about it, she doubted that Logan Graw would be upset with Jordan even if he kept her secret. And maybe she didn't even need to ask Jordan to do that. Would it really matter if her employer knew what her real last name was? It seemed unlikely that Collin could track her all the way here.

Then again, his job in cyber security had made it easy enough for him to hack into Mona's security systems and computers. How capable was he at searching for a person online?

"I'm not sure," she answered honestly.

Jordan raked a hand through his hair looking slightly frustrated. "Okay, but can you tell me this? There is something between us, right? I'm not alone in thinking that?"

Lanie jumped up. "No, you're not alone. Of course, you're not alone. Jordan, I like you."

Jordan got up too until he stood directly in front of her, and suddenly, his lips were on hers and he was kissing her with a fervor that he hadn't shown her since that very first kiss. His lips pressed against hers, demanding more from her, and Lanie could do nothing but open herself to the longing that had been hiding just below the worries in her subconscious.

With Jordan pressing her against him, the rush of excitement overpowered her other senses, and she gave in, wanting nothing more than to lean on Jordan and let him make things easier for just a moment.

And he did. His hands raked over her back, pulling her with him as he let himself fall back onto the couch. Lanie pulled her knees up until she straddled him, and then she stopped thinking and just let go.

There was more between them than passion now. It was an almost desperate need, Lanie's need to forget all the reasons that kept her from being able to envision a life with Jordan, and Jordan's frustration about not being able to have what he wanted, someone who was willing to commit to him fully.

He deserved better, but right now, Lanie couldn't get herself to stop kissing him. Not when his hands had wandered lower, cupping her bottom with gentle hands that urged her closer to him. Her body responded without her permission, pressing herself closer to him until it found the friction it needed. It was bliss, and Jordan's groan told her he felt the same way.

They could have tonight. Tonight, she was safe, and tonight would be for them.

* * *

Lanie looked into Jordan's face. With hooded eyes, he stared back, asking her a silent question. Did she want to keep going, or was there more he needed to know before they let things go any further?

"I can't promise you more than tonight," she said quietly. If she stayed with him tonight, they could share something amazing, but she knew he wanted more than a fling. He wanted more than one night. Still, she hoped he'd say yes.

For a moment, he looked torn. "I want you, Lanie, don't doubt that I do, but if you stay tonight, you have to promise me one thing. You'll tell me what happened before you came here and why you think you can't stay. I don't care if you think it'll affect my job or get me involved in whatever is going on. If you stay tonight, I need to know."

"Okay." He might think she was paying a price to stay when really, she was about to burden him with her problems. "I can do that."

Their mouths found each other again, and this time, Lanie let go of anything else. She allowed his kiss to give her absolution for her selfishness. All she wanted was to have this night with Jordan and give him everything she could. She wrapped her arms around him and tilted her head.

"You're beautiful," he groaned as his hands raked over

her back until they grabbed her bottom in a firm grasp.

Instead of replying, Lanie let her lips explore his neck, nibbling and kissing her way down and then up again, finding his earlobe and gently nibbling on it. One of his hands moved up her hip and over her waist until it moved even higher to find her breast, gently massaging her through her shirt.

"More," she gasped, and suddenly, they both pulled back, eager to remove the clothing that kept them apart.

Lanie pulled her shirt over her head and unclasped her bra. Her movements were rushed and clumsy, but she didn't care. Jordan's touch was gone, and she wanted it back as quickly as possible, lest the worries would return without it. He moved with the same fervency. They were both standing now, Jordan pulling his pants down until all he was wearing were his boxers. Lanie copied him, sliding her own pants down until they lay crumpled on the floor.

Outside, the sky opened, and the rushing and splattering of raindrops drowned out the noises of the birds and monkeys outside. Unlike the noise simulators she'd played to study to as a student, she now got to experience the real thing, a tropical rainstorm that kept the rest of the world out and let you focus on what was in front of you. And she wanted to experience so much tonight.

"Come," Jordan urged, pulling her toward the hallway. Lanie assumed he was bringing her upstairs to his bedroom, but he opened a door that led to the guest room, clearly too impatient to make it all the way upstairs. She would have followed him anywhere in that moment, the need inside her churning.

Lanie reached for him, pulling him against her. His skin felt hot against hers, but she pressed closer still. With the urging sound of the rain coming from outside, it felt as if her own blood were rushing faster through her veins.

She held herself back just a moment longer. "Are you sure?" she asked, needing the confirmation.

His eyes bore into hers, and he nodded. "I want you, Lanie, but only if you want me, too."

Her lips met his before she pulled back slightly to give him the reassurance he needed. "I want you, too." And the words rang true.

Something had drawn her to him from the very first day. This might not be how things worked in fairy tales, but she was no princess, and this felt so much better than waiting for the happily ever after that existed in stories but wasn't guaranteed in real life. This she could have, and she wanted it with everything in her.

He pressed himself against her until she stepped back

and stumbled onto the bed. Stretching himself out next to her, Jordan's hands wandered over her body while Lanie's went on an exploration of their own. It felt as if time had slowed. Cocooned into this house, surrounded by a rainstorm that would keep everyone in their homes, it was just them. Nothing could intrude.

Instead of the urgency from before, they now took their time discovering. She'd expected Jordan to be a fun lover, but the way he moved his lips over her skin felt like she was cherished and adored. The air was charged with passion and something akin to determination. He slid her panties down her legs and bared her to his view.

Maybe it was the seriousness she felt, but instead of a lighthearted one-night stand, they got lost in the nearness of each other.

When Jordan's mouth moved down her body, kissing around her belly button and then lower still, Lanie closed her eyes and let herself get lost in the sensations that followed. Her body sank into the bed as if she had lost the ability to move. Pinned down by sensations, Jordan teased her until all of a sudden, her muscles responded. She was at his mercy now, and her body clenched in waves of pleasure that only he controlled.

Lanie let herself go and drifted, trusting that Jordan

would keep her safe.

His kisses moved up her body then until he found her mouth, and she opened her lips, needing him to anchor her. He pulled her into his arms, and she snuggled against him while her body sensed his heartbeat and slowed its own frantic rhythm to meet his. She wanted to move again, to slide down his body and taste him the way he had done for her, but his arms tightened around her.

"Can you tell me why you came here and why you don't talk about your past much?" His voice was gentle, soothing, and she could feel the slight vibration in his chest as he spoke, her head snuggled into the groove just below his shoulder. It felt like she belonged in his arms, and she burrowed even closer into his embrace, his arms closing around her in response.

She wanted to keep exploring his body, but his arms held her pressed against him and she sensed he needed to hear her explain things more than he desired the passion between them. It told her so much about him that something in her chest ached.

Feeling safe and warm, she took a deep breath and told him how her life had changed so drastically before she'd come here. "I had a pretty good life back home. After I graduated with my master's degree, I got a job right away. I was lucky, but unfortunately, my friend's stalker came after me when she moved to get away from him after a violent attack. That's why I came here, and that's why I can't be sure I'm going to stay."

Jordan didn't speak for a moment, but she could tell his breathing had stopped and then sped up. His arm was now pressing her against him much tighter than was comfortable.

"You think he might find you here?"

"I can't be sure he won't." And that was the problem.

Without the throes of passion, she was able to recall the fear and worry much too quickly. Even if Collin would never find her, she'd always wonder if he'd show up the next day. If he'd try to do to her what he'd done to Mona.

Her friend had been a broken shell of herself after the attack. Lanie had never gotten to see whether Mona put the pieces back together because with whatever strength her friend had left back then, Mona had cut all ties and fled to be safe somewhere else. Lanie had to wonder if Mona felt as unsure about her choice as Lanie did.

Lying here with Jordan, Lanie could suddenly visualize what she might have if she could only let go of her past. A life with Jordan holding her. A new start with the man she'd fallen in love with.

Because she'd fallen for Jordan against all odds.

Except, with their passion interrupted by the reminder of reality, she knew for certain that coming here would never give her the new start she so desperately wanted. Even as she burrowed herself into the safety Jordan's arms offered, her rational mind still clung to the threat that it felt looming over her. The future she'd pictured was an illusion, one she couldn't even keep up long enough to spend one uninterrupted night with Jordan.

"But you came here to start a new life, right?" It was as if he'd been reading her thoughts.

She hoped he couldn't hear the desperation in her voice as she pressed her face closer into his chest. "I did. Except I don't know if it'll last."

"Then choose for it to last. You don't live alone, and it's unlikely that someone will rent a boat and arrive on the island without being noticed. I can make sure that if anyone unusual arrives at the airport, we'll be informed right away. I can help keep you safe so you don't need to worry all the time. Isn't that what you want?"

It was. But it wasn't *everything* she wanted.

She knew her slow reply gave her thoughts away. He wanted to be her knight in shining armor, but even with him by her side, she wouldn't be able to have a true happily ever after.

"It's not enough for you, is it?" he asked, his voice gruff now, though he still held her in his arms.

"I'll never see my family again, never speak to my best friend again, never work my actual job again. I'll never truly reclaim my freedom from him, and part of me will always feel like some of my life was taken from me." Tears accompanied the words that she'd never even allowed herself to think in the privacy of her own mind. They were the painful truth, and now he'd feel her pain as the wet droplets landed on his skin.

"What's your plan, then?" he asked, moving to sit up.

Lanie quickly wiped the tears away. Sitting up, she clutched the blanket to herself. It wasn't to hide herself from him—that would have been silly—but because his question made her feel exposed in a way she didn't like. Because she had no answer. Because it was the same question she'd been struggling with, and she hated that she couldn't give him or herself an answer. It made her feel weak, indecisive, and trapped. No blanket could solve those feelings, but she still clung to it now that Jordan had pulled away from her and she'd lost the contact that had given her strength.

"I don't know." Her voice came out sounding defeated, but when she looked up at Jordan, instead of the compassion she'd expected, she only saw that same neutral mask he'd put on earlier when she'd first told him she couldn't promise to stick around Howler Island forever. Except it was worse now because instead of his asking her to talk to him, she watched his expression close off completely.

It was worse because she was vulnerable now in a way she hadn't been before.

"So, you're not really here to build a new life. You're just saying that when really, you're ready to leave again, to return to your family or hide in the next location." It wasn't a question but an accusation, and Lanie felt her certainty that Jordan would understand her motivations, would understand her pain, waver.

He didn't look at all as if he understood. She'd told him her most painful secret just moments after he'd made her world explode, and now he was looking at her with a finality that bored itself into her chest.

"I want to build a new life here. I don't want to leave, but I might not have a choice." Except the words didn't feel true. If she had a choice, if she could freely decide where she wanted to live, wouldn't she return to her old life? A life with her family and the career she'd loved? Did she truly want to build a life here, or was it a back-up plan while she had no other options, a plan she'd give up once her circumstances changed?

"I see." Jordan stood then, pulling on his boxers. "And until this stalker arrives, even if he might never come, you'll always be ready to just take off. Is that right?"

She wanted to lie, to tell him she would overcome the worries the way she'd planned to, but she couldn't do that. Not after she'd made herself raw and vulnerable in front of him. Not if she didn't even believe in it herself. "I don't think I have another choice."

"Then I won't be a choice for you, either. I'm sorry, Lanie."

He didn't sound sorry at all. He sounded upset, and when he turned to walk out of the room, Lanie fought the sobs that tried to break free only long enough to pull on her panties.

When she went to the living room, Jordan wasn't there, so she quickly pulled on her clothes and left the villa, walking to the pier to call a water cab and leave Jordan behind.

He'd been unfair, and now she'd lost the one person who might have been worth starting anew for.

CHAPTER 11

Steady streams of tears painted trails down her cheeks, which, considering how awful Lanie felt, was only a tiny concession to her emotions. The man who was navigating the water taxi back to the main island did his best to avoid looking in her direction as she climbed out of his boat in Bocas. Lanie didn't care.

Her tears would dry, but would she ever be able to revive the hope that had made her think that rebuilding her life was possible? She'd done it all wrong.

Jordan had been understanding and willing to give her a chance, despite everything, and she'd given in to fear instead. Now, going home to a house she shared with two lovely women who had done nothing but nice things for her, all she could think about was that they weren't her family.

Having friends could never make up for the fierce

homesickness enveloping her. The thought of her mother and father made a sob escape her mouth as she left the water cab behind and headed down the street. In a few hours, she'd have to go back to work cleaning villas for people who came here to have the most incredible vacation of their lives. She'd once again have to try to shrink into the background when Jordan was around, but from now on, it would be so much worse.

Trying to make herself disappear had been hard before, but Lanie didn't think she could bear it if she returned and Jordan looked at her with that expressionless mask he'd worn earlier. Allowing herself to experience this selfish moment with Jordan today had been incredible, and now it was going to break her.

Her heart had just stopped aching from being torn from its home, and now she'd shattered it by destroying the one chance she'd had to rebuild.

By the time she made it to her room, the sky was already bright, and she just barely avoided running into Mama Lita and Gabriela. After a shower, she picked up her uniform. Whatever she felt right now, she had to go to work. Not because she cared about the job right now but because she couldn't slack off now that Jordan had told Logan Graw about them. If she called in sick after they'd had a fight and

Jordan's boss realized, she might get Jordan into trouble, and he didn't deserve that despite how he'd all but ripped out her heart earlier.

An unfamiliar ring tone sounded, and it took Lanie a moment before she realized it was coming from her dresser.

It was the burner phone her father had handed her the day she'd left them behind, telling her only to use it if she desperately needed to. He had memorized the number, never writing it down or saving it anywhere. His caution had only heightened her own anxiety at the time, and now, the phone was ringing.

She could see her hand tremble as she reached for the phone hidden underneath some shirts.

"Hello?" She was still caught in the tornado of her emotions, and the hope that she'd hear the familiar voice of her father made her throat so tight that she barely got the word out.

"Lanie? Oh, my God, Lanie!"

Lanie hadn't heard the voice on the other end of the line in months, but it was just as familiar to her as her own. "Mona?"

"Yes. Oh, Lanie, I'm so sorry. I'm so sorry I left you behind. I called your parents' place, and they told me you had to disappear, too. They gave me this number to call."

Mona was crying, and Lanie felt her own eyes well up again.

"Why are you calling? Are you safe?" Lanie walked the length of the room, pressing the phone to her ear.

What had happened that Mona was calling her?

Mona's sobbing stopped. "Oh, by the gods, yes. I'm sorry. All I'm doing is freaking you out more."

As much as she wanted to offer reassurances, Lanie didn't correct her friend. "Why are you calling, Mona?" Her voice came out sharper than she'd intended to, but after so much time living in a constant struggle against her own paranoia, she had to know what had happened for her father to give out this number.

"I'm home, Lanie. We decided to come home." Mona paused as if her statement was enough. Except it didn't explain anything.

"Why now? What happened?"

"When we went away, it was to be safe from him. From Collin. But Lanie, he haunted me no matter how often we moved. I went into therapy, and finally, I decided I wanted to return. My parents came too, of course. I didn't want them to live with the same fears I did."

"But what about Collin? Isn't he still out there?"

A moment of silence followed. "Yes, he is. He hasn't shown up so far, and we've done nothing to keep our return

206

a secret. If he is going to stalk me again, I just want to know as soon as possible, you know?"

The pain laced in Mona's voice told Lanie that no matter how brave her friend was trying to be, she still lived in fear. Except now, Mona had decided to face the threat head on rather than to play it safe. It was hard to decide whether she admired her friend for it or whether she wanted to call her out on being an idiot for taking unnecessary risks. Except Mona had never been an idiot. She'd been frightened, but she was strong and resilient, and she was brilliant.

"Oh, Mona." It was all she could say as she pressed her back against the wall and slid to the floor.

"I didn't know he came after you. Gods, Lanie, I'm so sorry I left you."

It was an unnecessary apology. It hadn't been Mona's fault that Collin was a psychopath who'd focused all his energy on Lanie when the initial target of his obsession had disappeared, but Lanie didn't tell her friend that. Mona's leaving had hurt her, even if she'd understood why her friend had to do it. Instead, she gave Mona what they both needed. Some reassurance.

"I'm okay, Mona. He never got too close." *Not like with you.* The thought hung in the air, reminding them both why Mona, and then Lanie, had fled their old lives.

It wasn't completely honest. She wasn't really okay. She was heartbroken, but at least right now, she was safe from Collin.

"So, you're coming home?" Mona asked, and Lanie should have expected the question, but instead, she felt confused by it. "Home?"

"Yes. I mean, even if Collin shows up again, he'd come after me now, right? So you can come back to your family. We can pick up where we left off and live our lives again."

Except Lanie had already picked up her life. Some of it, anyway.

As she looked around, she saw all the reminders that her life hadn't been on pause. Gabriela and Mama Lita weren't family, but they were her support, and they were her friends. The house she shared wasn't her own, but she loved living in the Caribbean with its rain, sunshine, and dolphins. However much she kept thinking that she wasn't able to move on without feeling completely safe from Collin's threat, somehow, she'd been moving forward all along.

The memory of Jordan's arms around her assaulted her mind before she could prevent it. The memory was even more painful now because it forced her to acknowledge the one thing that she hadn't wanted to admit.

She'd already made Bocas and Howler Island her home.

The entire time that she'd desperately tried to find a way to build a new life, she'd overlooked that she'd been well on her way toward doing just that. She'd liked her life before coming here. She'd had a rewarding career, friends, and her family, but she'd begun building the same here on the island. Maybe cleaning villas wasn't her dream job, but she could start working in marketing again if Mona was right and she was safe from Collin. Her parents didn't need to be replaced by new friends. They could visit.

Being here wouldn't have to be a backup plan. She could claim this new life she'd been building as hers and make it better because her family could become a part of it.

She could be with Jordan.

Except Jordan had told her he wasn't a choice for her anymore. He'd never trust her not to turn her back on him if she ever heard that Collin was back. Mona's return home wasn't the actual end of this mess.

Would Jordan believe her that suddenly, he was enough, and she wouldn't eventually regret her decision and return home to her family?

"I have to go, Mona. I'll call you soon." She hung up on her friend, knowing none of it was Mona's fault.

* * *

Jordan walked the jungle path all the way to Glamirante, the tiny community that was located on the other side of Howler Island. The path led through the nature reserve and should have calmed his racing thoughts, but he was still upset by the time the small school came into view. Only now, he was sweating too.

He'd done the right thing by walking away from Lanie.

Except it didn't feel right. It felt like he'd been a jerk.

She'd given him everything she could. He knew she had. She'd given him her honesty, and she'd given him her body. She likely would have given him even more of herself if he hadn't pulled the brakes, and the teenage voice in his head told him what an idiot he was for passing up that opportunity.

Watching Lanie come apart under his touch had been the hottest thing he'd ever witnessed, but when he'd kissed her and felt her trembling in his arms, she'd seemed so damn vulnerable that everything in him had wanted to protect her. And to do that, he needed to know her story.

Then she'd told him she was ready to walk away from him. That she had another life she'd return to once she could.

From what she'd hinted at before, he'd known she was afraid of something, but he'd never expected it to be a stalker. An actual person threatening her life. It hadn't seemed real when he heard it. Only now was the fact that she was here to hide from some maniac sinking in.

And he'd sent her on her way because like a kid, he still hadn't gotten over his daddy issues.

She wasn't like his dad, pretending to love him and planning a life together when she had no intention of following through with it. No, she was honest, but she was just as unwilling to commit to staying on the island with him as his father had been with his mother.

She didn't trust him to help her. She'd told him she'd rather go back to her old life if she got the chance.

He kicked at a rock that lay on the path. He'd acted like a jerk. He'd walked out on her when she was still naked in his bed, right after she'd shared her secret with him.

Lanie was hurting. He could see that. Still, she wasn't even willing to consider being with him, and that sucked. He shouldn't have hoped. He should have known better. It wasn't fair to expect her to give up her home and family when he himself was so tied to his own roots.

Despite the cool nightly temperature, the humidity in

the air had his shirt sticking to his body uncomfortably, but he couldn't care less.

There was only one way to say it. He was an idiot. A selfish idiot. He knew that, but it didn't make it any better.

Walking away from her was probably for the best because staying near her could only lead to one thing. He'd fall even harder for her. Lanie was everything he wanted in a partner. Except available. She wasn't that. Maybe she wasn't in a relationship, but she also wasn't ready for one, and didn't that just suck?

He sped up his steps. If he hurried, he could make it to the harbor in time for one of the fishing boats to give him a ride home. Not that there was anyone waiting for him.

Except when he arrived at the small dock the resort used for delivery boats and shuttles, there was someone waiting. Not for him, probably, but waiting, nevertheless.

"Hey, Jordan," Jane called as the fishing boat slowly sidled up against the pier. "Where are you coming from this early?"

It was only four thirty in the morning. He'd spent several hours hiking through the night, and he couldn't come up with a good excuse for where he'd been, so he just told her the truth.

"You went for a walk in the middle of the night?" Jane's

expression told him she thought he was crazy, though given that she too was currently standing at the pier, Jordan wondered whether she was in a good place to judge.

"And what brings you out so early?"

Jane's eyes brightened. "Well, actually, I think Lucy, one of the Howler females, is going to have her second baby any day now, and I really hope I'll catch sight of the troop so I can monitor how they react to having me around. Their interactions with humans have become fascinating over the last months, and I've decided to work up a research essay about it." Without waiting for Jordan's input, she ushered him off the pier.

As they walked up toward the welcome center, Jane told him more about the monkeys, though Jordan never quite figured out what she'd been doing at the pier.

"Anyway, you should come to breakfast at our place. Logan is always making enough for at least five people."

Given the choice between returning to his empty villa that might still hold Lanie's intoxicating scent and being fed at his friend's house, Jordan followed Jane to the private lane where Logan and his brothers each had bungalow style houses.

"Logan, look who I found," Jane announced.

"Please tell me you didn't bring home a monkey."

Logan's voice sounded concerned, and the corners of Jordan's mouth twitched upward.

"Depends," he called back. "Who are you more likely to feed, me or a monkey?"

Logan turned around from where he'd been scrambling some eggs. "Hey, man, what's up?"

"That's what I asked him, but he was being evasive," Jane announced, and Jordan stared at her back while Logan laughed.

"I went for a walk." Repeating his excuse sounded even worse than his first attempt at explaining why he'd been walking through the jungle in the middle of the night.

"Well, you're lucky Jane made me get up extra early to make breakfast." Logan loaded the kitchen counter with food, and they each claimed a bar stool.

There was no meat since Jane was a vegetarian, but it definitely beat cold cereal. While Jane gave Logan a report of her attempts at documenting the monkey's behavior when a new baby joined the troop, Jordan sat in silence and ate.

"So, what has you all brooding?" Logan finally asked.

"I'm not brooding, I'm eating."

"He looked like someone took his carving knives when he arrived at the pier," Jane interjected, and again, Jordan stared at her while Logan laughed.

"It's what I love best about her, her incredible observation skills and disregard for sugar coating anything." Logan wrapped an arm around his wife, and a pang of jealousy shot through Jordan.

"Come on, Jordan. Maybe we can help?" Jane offered, trying to redeem herself.

"Nothing you can help with, I'm afraid. Lanie isn't up for a relationship, and I'll just have to live with that."

Jane's eyes widened. "But why?"

Jordan looked at his empty plate. "Because she's afraid."

CHAPTER 12

"You've been moping ever since you disappeared with Jordan. If you don't want to tell me what happened, that's fine, but you've got to talk to him if you're this upset." Gabriela's patience was running thin, which Lanie couldn't fault her for.

About half an hour ago, Gabriela had called Lanie over to her room to get help deciding which dress to wear tonight, and so far, all Lanie had managed were distracted smiles and head shakes, depending on what she guessed was Gabriela's opinion on each dress. Perhaps she'd feel guiltier if Gabriela didn't look gorgeous in every single one of them.

She'd gone to work every day the past couple of weeks, never seeing Jordan and unsure why she hadn't taken the next flight home. It was obvious that Jordan was no longer interested, and she wanted to think he was the bad guy, but she knew that wasn't true. It would have been easier to blame him, but he wasn't a bad person, no matter how awful his rejection had hurt. Or how much it hurt to know he was avoiding her at the resort.

Having him walk away from her when she'd been naked in his bed, trusting him with her story, had been like a blow to her stomach, and she was most definitely mad at him. But she also remembered what he'd told her about his father, and it didn't take much to put two and two together. He wasn't callous. He was hurt.

Not that this realization had helped make the days go by any easier.

The only thing she'd done was call her parents. Her mother had cried at hearing her voice, but Lanie had been all out of tears. Somehow, her mother had known the exact right thing to say.

"It's fine, sweetheart. You've been through a lot. Take your time there. I'm sure you've made friends, and if you want, we can come to you once you're ready."

That had been over a week ago. Tonight was the midsummer party, and Jordan would have to be there. It would be her chance to talk to him. To apologize.

"If you don't go to him yourself and discuss whatever happened the other day, I will lock you two in the broom closet," Mama Lita announced from the hallway, much to Gabriela's amusement.

"I just bet they'd find a way to kill time in there."

Against her better judgment, Lanie blushed. She couldn't deny that her thoughts had gone back to the other night more than once, despite everything else on her mind. It had been amazing to feel Jordan's touch, and the idea of spending more alone time with him made her toes curl. Except if she ever got the chance to be with Jordan again, she'd be the one driving him mad with lust.

And she wouldn't walk away afterward.

"I was already planning on talking to him tonight. If he doesn't see me and run the other direction, that is." Seeing her fears confirmed sucked more than she wanted to admit. She knew she'd messed everything up, but his avoidance of her the past couple of weeks had made his disappointment in her painfully clear. She could only hope he'd listen to her tonight. It wasn't as if she hadn't always been honest with him.

"He'll listen." Once again, Mama Lita declared her opinion from the hallway, where she stood in her party dress, ready to go downstairs. "You two had better be downstairs in five minutes, or I'll tell everyone in the boat to take off without you."

Mama Lita would do it too, so Lanie quickly pointed to a purple flower dress Gabriela had favored earlier. "Wear that one."

In her own room, she put on the one dress she had that was appropriate for tonight's event. It was a Boho maxi dress with pink flowers printed on it. It had short sleeves, an A-line skater skirt, and a low-cut front. It wasn't anything overly fancy, but it did wonders for her figure, and she liked the soft swish of the skirt around her legs. It also wouldn't hurt if Jordan found her attractive when she tried to explain herself to him.

She only hoped that sometime between right now and arriving at the party, she'd come up with an idea of what exactly she wanted to say. Somehow, *sorry I downright refused to give us a chance even though we made out and I really like you* didn't sound like it would cut it. Especially since she couldn't quite decide what she hoped to get out of tonight's conversation.

Then again, her heart knew exactly what it wanted.

* * *

The bonfire was burning brightly, its smoke deterring the mosquitoes. The party was being held on the sand below the beach restaurant, and people moved between the fire and the bar, mingling and laughing. It was exactly how it was supposed to be, a fun evening for the Howler Island resort family to come together and have a night to enjoy just spending time together without any work.

Some older children were playing in the water while the younger ones, who had been allowed to miss their bedtime for this special occasion, were splashing in the pool. Their parents talked and danced to the live music.

Jordan watched Logan and Jane walk along the beach, lost in a private conversation the way couples in love did.

The past two weeks had gone by slowly. He'd wavered between apologizing to Lanie and deciding that it was best to let her think he was the jerk he'd acted like. How could he have walked out on her when she was vulnerable and lying naked in his guest bed?

Letting her think he had no regrets about the way he'd walked out on her would probably make things simpler for her. She could be angry at him, and once she felt safe, she could go home without looking back. It wasn't what he wanted, but it was the least he could do to make up for being an ass. She didn't need more to worry about, so he was taking himself out of the equation.

Of course, when he'd said as much to Logan and Jane

during dinner last night, Jane had given him a look and said he was one of the most clueless primates there were. Fortunately, she'd quickly gotten sidetracked lecturing them about a new study on the correlation of self-control and general intelligence in chimpanzees, which had been quite interesting and had distracted her from analyzing him any further.

That there was a common evolutionary history for human and primate self-control somehow stuck with him, and for the hundredth time that day, he considered whether he had enough self-control to just watch Lanie tonight or if he'd give in to his desire to apologize to her.

Someone tapped his shoulder, drawing his attention back to the party going on around him.

Gabriela stood there with a frown, but immediately, his eyes flew to both sides to see whether Lanie had come with her. She hadn't, and Gabriela shook her head at him, almost as if she were disappointed. Her frustration with him seemed uncalled for, given that he hadn't even seen her until this moment.

"She's getting a drink," Gabriela explained without having to ask what he was looking for. He shouldn't be surprised. The women lived together, after all, and Gabriela had witnessed that kiss they'd shared in front of Mama

221

Lita's house.

Forcing his head up and down in acknowledgment, Jordan focused his attention on Gabriela, trying to put on the smile that usually came so easily. "What can I do for you?"

"You can explain to me how you went from not dating any employees to turning Lanie into a moping mute." Her words were forceful, but her expression had turned soft. Gabriela hadn't grown up here, but after school, when her parents had kicked her out, she'd moved in with her aunt. Bart Graw had hired her a few months later, which meant they had known each other for a very long time, and he respected her opinions.

Jordan brought his hand to his neck, rubbing a spot that had begun to ache. "Things didn't quite work out."

"Yeah, apparently. She wants to talk to you, though."

Jordan stamped down on the hope that would only get him hurt.

If Lanie wanted to speak with him, he couldn't say no. They still had to work together. Unless, of course, she'd decided to leave and just wanted to hand in her resignation. Whatever she was planning, she deserved an apology. And truthfully, he wanted to talk to her too.

"If you see her first, can you ask her to meet me inside

the restaurant?" They needed some privacy, but he wasn't about to ask her to come to his house.

After giving him a warning look, Gabriela nodded and walked off. For a moment, Jordan wondered if Lanie even knew how much loyalty she'd already inspired in the friends she'd made here. Then he dismissed the thought and started his search.

Jordan passed by the bar and the people mingling around it, but he didn't spot Lanie, so he kept walking and opened the door to the restaurant. It was empty inside since everyone else had gathered around the pool and beach area. Heading into the kitchen, he took out two of the dessert plates that were stored there for later before turning back to go into the main room. Perhaps chocolate would make the conversation a little easier.

The side door he used earlier squeaked, and heavy steps sounded on the tiled floor.

* * *

By the time they joined the other partygoers, Lanie stopped playing with her skirt and moved on to pulling on a strand of her hair, first twirling it around her finger, then tugging on it. If she didn't speak to Jordan right away, she was liable to rip it out.

"I'm going to find Jordan first."

Gabriela nodded. "Thank God. You're no fun this anxious. At least after a few cocktails tonight, I might find out what even happened. I'll make sure to keep the Mojitos coming."

Lanie's nervous laugh probably served as further encouragement for Gabriela. "If you see him, can you send him my way? I'll check the bar first."

With Gabriela's agreement, Lanie turned her attention to the busy bar. There were quite a few familiar faces. A few people even greeted her by name. If she hadn't held back so much since arriving here, she could've made a lot more friends to tie her to this place.

She could have that now, if she chose to. She could be a member of this community of people who lived, worked, and celebrated together. Collin wouldn't come after her now that Mona was out of hiding. It felt like a selfish thought, but it had been Mona's choice. Maybe she should feel compelled to return and be by her best friend's side, but deep down, Lanie knew the truth. Something in her had shifted since she'd arrived here.

She wanted to stay, wanted this place to become her home, not because she had to hide but because she loved it here. Maybe she could freelance for the tourist shops and take on marketing clients. And when her parents visited, she could take them to Cacao Playa.

There was only one thing she couldn't choose because it wasn't her choice to make. She needed to tell Jordan what she wanted, and then it was up to him to tell her if he wanted her, too.

A wave of nerves washed over her. His rejection had stung, and she wasn't even sure he'd let her explain things now.

Turning in a circle, Lanie looked for something to anchor her. Jordan was nowhere in sight, but the ocean glistened in the evening sun, and the music and laughter that surrounded her calmed her frayed nerves. Near the water, children were playing, and her feet carried her in that direction, maneuvering her way through the tight dance crowd.

The sand made its way into her sandals, forcing her to bend down and pull them off. Righting herself, she saw Logan and Jane coming toward her. After what happened with Jordan, the resort owner might recognize who she was, and Lanie considered turning away, unsure how to act.

"Lanie?" It wasn't Logan who called out her name but Jane.

"Uh, yes?" She could hardly ignore them now. She closed the distance, her sandals swinging from her fingers, the warm sand massaging her feet.

"It's great to properly meet you," Jane announced, her husband standing next to her, his expression friendly but reserved.

What had happened to her plan to stay as anonymous as possible? Perhaps it had all been pointless, anyway. Whatever the case may be, the friendly woman in front of her made Lanie smile. "It's nice to meet you, too, Dr. Graw."

"Oh please, it's Jane, and I actually kept my last name, so it's still Holland."

Silenced by her outdated assumption that Jane **would have** taken her husband's name, Lanie looked between the two. Logan's hand was behind Jane's back, and they stood close together, despite the evening heat that made Lanie's skin feel slightly damp.

"I think Jordan is looking for you," Jane said, the words sounding excited and slightly rushed.

Logan's warning, "Jane," was drawn out and more a hum than a contribution to the conversation. He apparently didn't share Jane's enthusiasm.

"Oh, don't Jane me. You know as well as I do that he

wants to speak with her." The eye roll that accompanied the statement **would have** made Lanie laugh if her insides hadn't just done an excited jump that left her slightly breathless.

"Well, I'd better go find him then," she offered and got a firm nod back from Jane. Logan simply watched her for a moment before he nodded with an unreadable expression.

Turning back to the pool and bar area, Lanie once again scanned the crowd until she spotted Gabriela, who waved her over.

"Jordan went to the restaurant."

Thanking Gabriela, Lanie quickly walked toward the restaurant's beach entrance. If she took too much time, she'd just get more nervous. She knew what she wanted to tell him now. There wasn't anything she could do but convince him to listen.

Opening the door, she heard male voices. The sound felt like someone had slapped her across the face.

She knew those voices.

The warm baritone belonged to Jordan, but that other voice was one she'd heard in her nightmares too many times.

Collin was here, and he'd found Jordan.

She wanted to turn around and run away, to yell for someone to get help, but that hadn't worked for Mona, and it wouldn't work now. Collin was good at manipulating what people saw. His intelligence was the scariest thing about him because it meant it had taken too long to prove that he'd been after Mona. The only thing that had gotten him to implicate himself was when his disgusting urges had made him abandon caution.

It was the only option she had, and terror rushed through her.

She wasn't strong enough. She'd been paranoid and afraid for so long that the thought of confronting Collin made her blood freeze, preventing her from moving. This man had taken so much from her, and now he was talking with Jordan. Did he know Jordan and Lanie had been spending time together? Had he been watching them all along? What would he do when he saw her?

She couldn't allow someone else to be harmed because of him.

Especially not Jordan.

She loved him.

The warmth of the thought allowed her to slowly inch forward.

Making her way toward the short hallway that connected the kitchen and the restaurant, where she heard the men talk, Lanie looked around for a weapon. There was nothing except a wooden carving of a palm tree that decorated the wall. She immediately recognized it as one of Jordan's pieces, but that didn't matter now. As silently as she could, she took the carving off the wall. It was about the size of her lower arm, too big to hide.

When she almost reached the corner, her racing heartbeat that had drowned out any noises before suddenly calmed, and she could make out what Jordan was saying.

"As I said, we don't have a Lori working for us, so perhaps you should return to your hotel and double-check the information you have. We have a private event going on, so I won't be able to help you today, anyway." Despite the polite words, Lanie heard the edge in Jordan's voice. Hopefully, Collin didn't hear it. Had Jordan realized who he was talking to? That Collin was looking for her?

It wouldn't be enough to get Collin to back off. She needed to get him to lose his temper.

"Perhaps the name Lorraine rings a bell? Sometimes she uses her full name. I rather think my information is accurate, and since you're the manager, it seems that you ought to know the people you recently hired."

Lanie stepped around the corner. Jordan's eyes widened when he saw her, alerting Collin that someone had come up behind him. She had to force herself to stay in place when Collin turned around and gave her a slow perusal.

"Well, look who's here, after all. It's good to see you, Lori." The smile he gave her might have looked friendly to anyone who didn't know Collin, but she could see the hatred in his gaze. He still blamed her for Mona's rejection.

He turned toward her fully now, obviously not caring what Jordan thought.

This wasn't like him. Something about Collin seemed less polished. Less put together. Scarier. Maybe prison had broken some of his carefully maintained façade he'd never let go of before, even during his trial.

"You found me," she said, hating that her voice shook. "What are you doing here, Collin? Don't you have any prison buddies you need to visit?" The words tumbled out before she could rethink her plan.

Behind Collin, Jordan's eyes widened even further. She shook her head slightly at him, moving her eyes to the entrance area in a silent hint, hoping Collin wouldn't notice. Of course, Jordan couldn't understand why she had to rile

Collin up. She could see the worry in his eyes when Collin walked toward her. Still, Jordan gave her a tiny nod.

Not trying to be subtle, Jordan moved toward the door that led to the beach bar. "Well, if this is who you were searching for, it sounds like this is a personal conversation. I'll get back to the party . . . unless I'm needed here?" He raised an eyebrow, giving her one last chance to stop him.

Collin ignored Jordan completely, not moving his eyes away from Lanie. She shook her head, feeling cold rush through her, and Jordan kept walking until he was hidden in the entrance area.

When the restaurant door opened and closed, her heart sank for a moment. She wanted him to be safe, but she'd need a witness. Had he misunderstood and actually left? A second later, Jordan peaked around the corner, and she knew he hadn't truly gone outside.

When she focused on Collin again, he was smiling at her. Her eyes had only darted away from him for a second to follow Jordan's movement, and with his back to the door, Collin was obviously convinced that Jordan had left.

He'd always been good at deceiving people and didn't seem to suspect that Jordan knew who he was. It was hard to believe that even after being convicted once, Collin still assumed he had the believable persona of a professional security expert who could easily find a woman interested in him, not someone who would ever be suspected of stalking.

Fear made her throat close now that she actually had to speak to Collin, but somehow, she managed to push her accusations through. "I knew you were pathetic when you started dating Mona, but are you really so sad that you have to follow me around the world just so you can justify to yourself that no woman in her right mind would want to not be with you? I know you're a cruel sadist after what you did to Mona, but I had no idea that you're stupid, too."

Rage flared up in Collin's eyes. He wasn't used to being confronted like this, and they both knew it. With Mona, he'd worn her down so much that by the time they had realized Collin was behind it all, she had been too frightened to stand up to him. Nobody in Collin's life had believed he was capable of the things he'd done. He was too good of an actor.

Except Lanie had disliked him from the start. And he'd known and blamed her for it ever since. He even held her responsible for Mona's breaking up with him.

Confronting him now was the only way she could think of to get him to show who he really was. It was the only chance she had to stop this new horror before it started again, but as he visibly tried to rein in his hatred, all she could see was Mona, lying in the hospital bed, her face beaten and her eyes red from too much crying.

Lanie took a step backward, further into the restaurant. She was still clinging to the carving that grew heavy in her hand. Collin's eyes followed her, and when he noticed her makeshift weapon, something in his expression shifted. Instead of growing more cautious, he advanced on her, and she realized he didn't see an opponent.

He saw his prey retreating, frightened.

It excited him.

She wanted to tell Collin that he needed to stop what he was doing, that it was madness. She wanted to yell that Jordan should get help, but she clamped her lips shut. She couldn't tell Collin that Jordan was watching, couldn't risk that someone came now, when they had nothing against Collin that would stop him from stalking her again. Instead, she allowed a tear to run down her cheek. It wasn't hard. She was terrified of what was to come, but that fresh sign of her weakness spurned Collin on even more.

"What are you doing here, Lori, huh? Did you think you could just ruin my life and then take off and hide? You should know better. I'll always find you."

"You couldn't find Mona when you got out of prison. Isn't that why you made do with me? Looks like you always have to settle. Never get what you want, do you?"

She knew the words would trigger him, but instead of lunging for her, he merely smiled. "Ah, yes, my little Mona hid for a little while, didn't she? But she came home to me now. I knew she would eventually."

A fear so overwhelming, she barely managed to stay upright took over. "What did you do to her?" She hadn't spoken with Mona since their one phone call, and the guilt she now felt made a wave of nausea wash over her.

Collin chuckled even though his body was tense, and hatred flared in his eyes. "Still pretending to care for her, are you? You don't need to bother with me. We both know better. You've always been jealous of her, poisoned her against me because I chose her and not you. I can see that now."

Behind Collin, Jordan observed the exchange. He had silently stepped back into the main room, obviously not wanting to be too far away if Lanie needed his help. She could tell it was taking all his willpower not to step in, but he must have sensed that she needed to do this. She shook her head again. She needed him to let this play out. Still, the knowledge that he was here, ready to help her, steeled her resolve.

"What do you want from me then?" she asked Collin, who was too far gone in his rage to pay attention to his surroundings. It was obvious that he'd lost touch with reality. The intelligence that had made him dangerous before was gone now, replaced with a display of the evil he'd been hiding. He was exactly where she wanted him, and that was terrifying.

As if her question reminded him that he had a plan, Collin took another step toward her. "I'm going to make sure that this time, you won't come between us."

Her plan had made sense before. But now that Collin was closing the distance between them, it was hard to recall that this was the only way they could get him arrested, the only way to prevent him from coming back day after day, night after night, always waiting for the right moment to hurt her.

She prayed that the cameras in the restaurant were recording, otherwise all they would have were their witness accounts.

When Collin reached for her, she stepped back further. Enticed by the hunt, he lunged forward, and she reflexively swung the carving. The wood hit his arm, and she lost her hold on it. The noise as it landed on the floor was deafening in her ears.

Then Collin's hand grabbed her shoulder, his grip painfully tight. "Let's go, Lori. We're going to chat elsewhere. No need to disrupt the party with your screams."

Panic shot through her. This wasn't enough. No judge would convict him for just grabbing her, and if she went with him anywhere, she might not be able to come back at all.

Collin's hand on her shoulder didn't loosen as he turned around to walk her out. Before she could kick at him, Jordan stepped in front of Collin.

"I don't think so." Jordan's face barely contained his anger. "Let go of her now."

CHAPTER 13

The psycho had his hand on Lanie's shoulder, and her pained expression was evidence that he wasn't being gentle. No surprise there, and still, Jordan's anger almost made him snap.

This was the man who'd sent Lanie running from her home. From her family. Never had he looked at a stranger feeling as much hatred as he did right now. Hearing Lanie tell him she had gone into hiding because she was afraid and actually seeing this sociopath hurting her were two very different things, and Jordan wasn't sure he could control his anger another moment longer.

"I'll only say this one more time. Let go of her." He forced his voice to stay calm. He needed to stay in control to make sure Lanie wouldn't get hurt.

The guy had the nerve to laugh. If Jordan hadn't listened to the hate he'd been spewing at Lanie just moments earlier, he might have believed that the psycho was perfectly at ease. This was a man who had no qualms about hurting a woman.

"Hey, no need to worry. We were just leaving. Lanie here will be perfectly safe with me. You'll see her bright and early on Monday morning." The way Collin emphasized Lanie's name made Jordan clench his hands.

Lorraine. Lori. Lanie. He hadn't even known her real name until now, but that didn't matter anymore. He knew what truly mattered. She was a kind and honest person who should never be hurt. He'd fallen for her, and now he wanted to protect her with every fiber of his being.

"If that's so, you won't mind letting go of her now, right?" He wanted to lunge for the guy, rip his hands off Lanie, but he didn't know what Collin was capable of. What if he had a weapon? It wasn't like Jordan had any experience with fighting. Lanie was better off if he tried to keep the situation calm.

Anger flashed across Collin's face. Apparently, the psycho didn't care about keeping up his façade anymore. "Just get out of my way, man. This doesn't concern you."

Jordan didn't move. He needed to keep Collin from escalating the situation until Logan managed to get some of the men rounded up to step in. Lanie had told him this guy had been violent with her friend, and given her trembling voice when she'd told him, he didn't take the account lightly. Better if they got backup.

Right now, Lanie seemed to be caught in some internal dilemma. She wasn't making eye contact, instead staring at a point behind him. He didn't know what she'd tried to do earlier, but he suspected that she needed to face her fears and confront this guy on her own. He could understand that, but the second the brute had lunged for her, Jordan had lost his patience. It was good for Lanie that she was brave enough to want to deal with this sociopath, but he cared too much for her to let her be harmed.

"Look, you're welcome to leave, but Lanie is attending our party, and I rather think she wants to stay. So why don't you just let go of her, and if she wants, she can give you a call?" If he could get this guy out of here for now, they could get Lanie to safety and then get the police involved.

Instead of looking relieved that he was helping, Lanie suddenly shook her head. She was trying to be subtle, but this time, the movement caught Collin's eye. She'd pushed her luck one too many times.

When Collin's grip tightened even further, Lanie winced. "Oh, but Lanie doesn't want to stay for a boring party when we have so much catching up to do."

The guy was obviously not in his right mind anymore. Avoiding Jordan, Collin pulled Lanie to the other side of the room where a staircase led to the street exit.

He couldn't let them leave. Not when he wasn't sure that help was waiting outside. But before he could act, Lanie started laughing. It wasn't happy laughter but a hysterical sound coming from a woman who was obviously reaching the limit of what she could bear. The sound was so startling that even Collin stopped to see what was going on.

"Like any woman would want to spend time with you, Collin!" Lanie's laughter increased.

What the heck was she doing?

"I bet you didn't even get lucky in prison. Not even the criminals would've wanted to touch you, am I right?"

Collin's knuckles turned white on her shoulder, and Lanie's pained gasp was the last straw. Jordan took the steps between them in a sprint, but before he could reach them, Collin had plunged his fist into Lanie's face. All he could see was Lanie's body hitting the ground, the noise of her head hitting the floor loud enough to give him nightmares for years.

Then Jordan reached Collin and his own fist flew.

It hurt. He'd never actually hit someone. Mock fights with Logan and Ben had never involved the force he'd put into hitting Collin, and it stung. At least it really was true that the other guy looked worse. Collin's nose was obviously broken, blood gushing out. But the psycho was still on his feet and ready to retaliate.

Jordan lifted his fists. He'd do whatever it took to keep this guy from hurting Lanie again, but luckily, in that moment, both doors to the restaurant opened and Logan and several resort workers rushed in, all ready to help.

His best friend had gotten his text and had known what to do.

* * *

Lanie's world was still fuzzy when Jordan bent down to her.

"Lanie? Lanie, can you hear me?"

Her eyelids were too heavy to lift and there was pain in her head and her left hip. The floor was hard, and the only thing she really wanted was something to make the pain disappear.

"Logan! We need to get her to a doctor." Jordan's voice sounded panicked.

She didn't want to move. Moving would hurt, she was sure of that. She wanted a pillow. Something to make the ground less hard.

Then darkness took over again.

When Lanie woke up, she was in a soft bed. Her head still hurt, but she could open her eyes now. The room was familiar, but not her own. It was the same guest bedroom she and Jordan had been in the day he'd rejected her. She really didn't want to like it here, but it was cozy. The large queen bed with the light comforter she was lying beneath stood opposite the door, while beautifully carved wooden flowers hung all over the wall opposite the window. Outside, she could make out the tops of some young palm trees.

When she turned, pain reverberated in her head, but she pushed herself up anyway. On the nightstand she found a glass of water and a package of pills with a sticky note. *Take two.* Reading the label, she confirmed the pills were for headaches, and she greedily swallowed them. Once that was accomplished, another need made itself known.

When she tried to roll out of bed, a sharp pain pierced through her hip and a loud groan escaped her. This so wasn't okay.

"Lanie?" Jordan asked from the door. "Can I come in?"

"Sure," she croaked, fighting a wave of nausea. By the time Jordan stood in front of her, she'd managed to get into a seated position on the edge of the bed. Before either of them could say a word, Gabriela walked in looking almost as concerned as Jordan did.

"I really need to use the bathroom." Maybe she'd be embarrassed under different circumstances, but her bladder was too full to worry about anything else.

Pushing past Jordan, Gabriela came up to her. "Here, let me walk with you."

Together, they made their way to the bathroom across the hall. Lanie was certain she could have managed by herself, but Gabriela hadn't budged when she'd said so, and Lanie didn't have any time to argue.

Minutes later, she'd emptied her bladder and washed her face, feeling a lot better. She was still wearing her party dress, except instead of pretty makeup, her face was now decorated with an ugly red bump near her hairline and a dark purple bruise under her left eye.

The memories rushed back now that her body's immediate needs were taken care of, and she suddenly felt dizzy, clinging to the wall for support.

"Lanie? Are you okay?" Gabriela called from outside the door.

She had to pull herself together. She was safe right now. The rest she could figure out later. "I'm okay. I just got a little dizzy."

A curse came from outside, and the next second, Jordan barged in. "Here, let me get you back to bed."

"No, please. Can we sit on the couch?" She didn't want to feel like an invalid. Not when the memory of Collin's appearance had already made her feel vulnerable.

When Jordan agreed and brought her to the couch, sitting down next to her, Gabriela excused herself to make some tea.

"What happened? Why am I here? Where is Collin?" Lanie's questions came out one after the other.

Why couldn't she remember?

"You hit your head pretty hard when Collin hit you." The way Jordan clenched his jaw after the sentence was enough evidence that despite his gentle tone, he was anything but calm. Luckily, he swallowed once and then continued speaking. "The doctor examined you, but you kept drifting in and out of consciousness. He said you'd be okay staying here, though, and Logan gave him the empty villa next door so he could come and check on you intermittently. Otherwise, we would've airlifted you to the hospital. He said something about your being in shock. I already messaged him, and he'll be here in a minute. He still wants to check you for a concussion."

Five minutes later, the doctor walked in. Jordan had summarized what had happened after she'd been hit, and Lanie still couldn't believe that Collin had actually been arrested. Not only had Jordan gotten Logan and some of the workers to help secure Collin after he'd assaulted her, but he'd also made sure that the local police ran Collin's name. Since he had violated the terms of his probation, they were currently holding him until a judge could investigate his case on Monday.

"You definitely have a light concussion, and your hip is bruised, but you'll be okay in no time," the doctor assured her after he'd performed several tests.

"Anything we can do to make things easier for her?"

"She needs rest to let her brain recover." He turned to Lanie. "Avoid anything that makes your symptoms worse. If you feel dizzy or nauseous, take it easy, and call me if anything persists over the next couple of days. No work for two weeks, and I want to see you in my office on Wednesday."

Lanie nodded before realizing that the movement was a bad idea. "Of course."

She watched as Gabriela walked the doctor to the door. When she looked back at Jordan, he was staring at her.

"What is it?"

"You wanted this, didn't you?" A level of incredulity sounded in his voice. "You wanted him to hurt you so we could get him arrested."

"It worked, didn't it? I just hope this time, there is more we can do to keep him monitored or locked up in the future."

Jordan's expression shifted. "You're braver than I could ever give you credit for, you know that?" Then he leaned forward and his lips met hers. "You scared me, Lanie. Please don't ever do that again."

She laughed, but the throbbing in her head got even worse, so instead, she reached up to cup his cheek. "I won't. There's only this one stalker I didn't tell you about."

Jordan's lips twitched upward. "Well, there's a relief."

Just as Gabriela walked back into the room, someone knocked on the front door.

Jane and Logan walked in, and immediately, Jane's hand flew to her mouth. "Oh, Lanie!"

"That bad, huh?" She'd already seen the bruise and bump on her face, so it didn't exactly come as a surprise that she wasn't about to win a beauty pageant in the coming weeks, but what was surprising was that the resort's owner and his wife had come by.

Would she get in trouble for using a fake name on her employment papers?

"Jordan told us some of your story, and you must have been going through hell," Logan offered, and Lanie relaxed slightly.

"It wasn't easy, but I'm still so sorry to have lied to all of you." She turned to Jordan and then Gabriela.

Her friend shook her head. "Don't even apologize. You obviously had a good reason."

"It's good of you to stop by, but the doctor wants Lanie to rest. Perhaps you could come back tomorrow?" Jordan spoke up, and Logan gave him a nod.

"I'll come by tomorrow with some food," Jane offered. "I know Jordan can't cook for the life of him."

Lanie bit her lip. It wasn't a usual habit, but how could she explain to Jane that she couldn't stay at Jordan's place, however much she might want to? They needed to talk, yes, but she wouldn't force herself on him. Unlike Gabriela, he hadn't immediately waved off her apology. "Well, I think I'll go back to Mama Lita's house today, but if you don't mind coming to Bocas, then I'd love a visit." It was the most diplomatic answer she could offer, and it truly would be good to have another friend on the island.

"No, you won't." Jordan's voice sounded almost angry. "You need to lie down and rest."

Seeing her worried look, his voice gentled. "If you'd rather not stay with me, maybe Gabriela can stay here with you. I can move to one of the rental villas for a couple of nights."

Her heartbeat sped up when she took in Jordan's concerned but determined expression. It looked like he truly wanted her to stay with him, as if he wasn't just inviting her to stay because he felt it was the right thing to do. "No, no. I mean, I don't mind staying with you. I just don't want to impose. You know, after everything."

Nobody had left, watching the exchange with interested expressions.

"Lanie," Jordan started, but then he shook his head in frustration. "Is that what you want me to call you? Or do you want us to call you Lorraine or Lori now?" He looked almost pained when he used the nickname Collin had called her.

"Please call me Lanie. It's what my grandmother always called me."

His smile felt like a little reward, like he acknowledged that she hadn't completely lied to him. She had given him something of her past, after all. "Okay. Lanie. You aren't imposing. I want you to stay. I've always wanted you to stay. You should know that."

The words pierced her heart, and she ignored Gabriela's squeal. "I want to stay, too."

"You can recover here in my house for as long as you want." Jordan moved to sit closer to her and gently took her hands in his. "Whatever you want to do, I'll respect it, but before you make up your mind about me, you need to know that I'm so sorry about the way I acted before. I was hurt and lashed out. I won't make that mistake again. I'm here whenever you need me."

Her hip hurt, and her head was still aching with a dull pain despite the meds, but suddenly, Lanie felt daring. Collin wasn't completely taken care of yet, but she'd faced him, and now she felt ready to take a leap of faith. "And what if I never want to leave?"

"Then you'd make me very happy."

The way Jordan was looking at her made her want to cry. After the stress of the past year, she finally felt like she'd made it across a huge hurdle, and now her emotions were all over the place. She was overwhelmed and exhausted, but looking into Jordan's eyes soothed and centered her somehow. The tears pricking her eyes weren't tears of sadness, anger, or exhaustion, but grateful tears because after everything she'd witnessed and experienced with Collin, she was still capable of trusting and loving a man.

"Tell her, Jordan," Jane urged, and Gabriela giggled.

Jordan ignored them. Without moving his eyes from hers, Jordan said, "Logan, get everyone out, please."

"Lanie?" Logan asked before following Jordan's request.

She smiled. "Yes, please."

A moment later, they were finally alone.

"How are you feeling?"

She didn't want to talk about the aches in her body. She wanted to have the conversation with him that had brought her into the restaurant. "I'm fine, but Jordan, I need to explain."

He nodded and reached up to brush a strand of her hair back. "You don't need to explain for me, but I'm happy to listen."

She smiled gratefully. "When I came here it was because I had to, and it took me a long time to figure out what I actually wanted. Collin's showing up is only part of that. I like being here, and I've decided I want to stay. I have

250

a degree in marketing, and I'm going to see if I can do freelance work for some of the tourist businesses in the area. I'll ask my parents to visit me, too, so I can see them."

Jordan's thumb stroked over the back of her hand, the contact more encouraging than he could ever know.

"I didn't walk away from my old life because I was unhappy with it. I was actually really happy until Collin showed up, but somehow, being here made me realize I want to open a new chapter in my life. I have no guarantees for you, but I can promise you that I truly want to start building a life here and . . ."

Her words faltered until Jordan smiled at her. "And?"

"And I'd gladly go on another date with you, if you'll still have me."

He leaned forward and gently pressed his lips to hers.

"I want that, too."

EPILOGUE

Jordan walked up the stairs to Lanie's small home.

Luckily, over the past six months, she'd secured several clients in the area, including doing some work for the resort, so she hadn't resorted to renting an apartment over one of the bars. He thanked the stars for that every time he came here, though that wasn't all that often since they spent most of their nights at his place. Listening to a bunch of drunken tourists party all night just wasn't particularly romantic, nor relaxing.

He knocked and waited for Lanie's response before stepping into the small hallway that was decorated with three of his carvings. Two of them had been his housewarming gifts. One depicted a dolphin, while the other was a beach scene with two hammocks that she said reminded her of the day they'd spent at Cacao Playa. There was also the carving of a palm tree that used to hang in the restaurant. She'd told him it was a reminder to herself that she had the inner strength to always stand up for herself and the people she loved.

"Are you ready?" he called just as Lanie walked out of her bedroom looking absolutely beautiful.

"I am. Are you finally going to tell me where we're going for our date?"

He shook his head. "Nope." He walked toward her and wrapped her soft body in his arms. Then he claimed a kiss.

When they pulled apart, he grinned at her. "Come on, we don't want to miss our boat."

Soon after Collin's attack, Lanie had moved out of Mama Lita's place and rented this small house in Bocas. She'd been firm that living on her own for a while was a step that she'd needed to take as part of her recovery from the paranoia that the stalking had caused her to live with for far too long.

"Aren't we taking your boat?" Lanie asked, obviously suspicious.

"That's right, and the captain wants to make sure we leave quickly."

Her laughter made him smile the way it always did. He'd fallen in love with Lanie incredibly fast, but over the past six months, he'd learned more and more about her that confirmed what his instincts had told him right away. Lanie was the woman he wanted to be with.

Now he simply needed to convince her to speed things up. Just a bit, anyway.

Lanie grew more suspicious when he steered his boat toward Howler Island. "I thought we were going on a date, not to your place."

"We are going on a date. You just have to be patient for a little longer, and then you'll find out what the plan is. Consider yourself kidnapped."

He jumped onto the dock and tied his boat to a metal ring with a wide grin.

Lanie's smile grew as she took his hand to step out onto the dock. "Well, I did just read this rather steamy romance novel about a pirate who kidnapped an innocent Scottish lady."

Jordan laughed. "That book sounds like it was more about plundering and ravishing and less about romance and dating."

Lanie's snort was anything but ladylike. "Well, the author wrote the book, and I consented to indulging in the fantasy. Plus, I had candles burning while I read."

"Well, in that case, let the plundering begin." He wrapped his arms around her and ravished her mouth in the best pirate impression he could muster.

When he leaned back again, Lanie looked sufficiently mussed. "There, now you look like a lady who's been introduced to the sinful pleasures of the sea."

An amused coughing interrupted them when Gabriela stepped onto the dock with a basket. "Here you go. Wouldn't want any pirates to starve to death, though it looks like you've got your treat already picked out, Jordan."

Lanie's face took on a rather adorable shade of red, and Jordan couldn't help laughing again. "Thank you. And tell Mama Lita thanks for the food."

"Tell her yourself. If you don't visit her soon, she's going to hunt you down, anyway."

"Fair enough. I'll see you tomorrow!" He tugged on Lanie's hand, pulling her past Gabriela and past the welcome center to the road that led to the building used by Jane's non-profit organization.

Behind the compound, a small path led into the jungle, and he grinned when Lanie looked at him with wide eyes.

"Jane hasn't shown you this place yet?" He'd hoped so, but he wasn't sure since Jane and Lanie had become good friends over the past few months. Even with all the preparations for today, he hadn't remembered to ask Jane.

"No, she's never brought me here. We mostly meet at the beach or go to get cocktails so we can talk about you and Logan," Lanie teased.

Together, they made their way along the narrow jungle path. When they reached the lookout that the primatologists used to study the local monkeys, Lanie's face broke into a huge smile. Astonished, she took in the flower garlands that were wrapped around the platform that was nestled high into the treetops.

"This is beautiful!"

Jordan had borrowed some of the decorations Jane had used to transform this place on her wedding day, and the result was spectacular. He and Gabriela had worked on it all morning.

"Why don't you climb up while I lift the basket up with the pulley?"

By the time Jordan climbed up to the platform, Lanie was already sitting on one of the two pillows he'd brought up earlier. Luckily, none of the monkeys had stolen them.

"This is a lot better than being kidnapped," Lanie said, looking completely relaxed. Her dark hair hung over her shoulders in loose waves, and her face was free of any makeup. None of the tension she'd used to display before Collin's attack remained now, and Jordan loved seeing her like this.

Loved her.

He moved his pillow so they could sit next to each other.

"Are you excited for Mona to get here tomorrow?"

Lanie looked thoughtful. "I really am. We have a lot to talk about. I hope we can get back to the friendship we used to have."

After the police had released Collin from their custody, he'd gone to Canada, where he'd attempted to get close to Mona. He hadn't known that she had a security team who watched over her ever since her parents had learned about Collin's attempt to get to Lanie. Injured in the resulting fight, he was now back in prison, this time without a chance of early release.

"Do you think she holds it against you that you stayed here?"

Lanie shook her head. "No, I don't, but I sometimes feel a little guilty."

He wrapped his arm around her, enjoying the feel of her snuggling closer. "You'll have two weeks together. You've been friends for so long, I'm sure you'll be able to talk through everything."

He could feel her nodding against his shoulder. "Yeah, you're right. But tonight is for us. What food did you bring us?" she asked, sitting up straight again.

They'd quickly come to terms with the fact that neither of them was any good at cooking and usually made do with simple meals, but for today, he'd talked Mama Lita into making them something special.

"We have some fried yucca roots, a primavera salad, and some Almojábanos." Lanie had developed a taste for local dishes, which Jordan could only support, especially when they were homemade by Mama Lita.

"Oh, and are those Tostones in that container over there?" Lanie all but pushed him off the platform in her attempt to reach for the pieces of fried plantains. It was never a good idea to get between a woman and her dessert.

After he pulled out two glasses and poured them each some wine, they started eating. Lanie told him about her day at work and the plans she'd made for Mona's visit while Jordan listened, waiting for his opportunity.

"You've been kind of quiet today," Lanie said, apparently not oblivious to his distraction.

"Well, I actually want to talk to you about something."

When Lanie just raised her eyebrows, he continued, "I thought that maybe you and Mona would want to stay in my villa while she visits. Mona could have her own guest bedroom, and you could use the resort's amenities."

"That would be amazing. And I suppose I could just come and stay with you every night, huh?" Her smile told him she liked the idea as much as he did.

"Thank you," she added and leaned over to kiss him.

When her lips touched his, he all but forgot that he wasn't quite done yet. He'd been wanting to ask Lanie this for a while now, so he pulled back, only to give her another gentle peck on the lips. Then he tried his luck. "I also thought that when Mona leaves, maybe you'd like to stay and keep living in the villa."

When Lanie didn't immediately answer, he quickly continued, "I know you needed some time to live on your own, and I completely understand that. Actually, I'm really proud of you for it, but I love you, Lanie, and it would make me incredibly happy if you'd come and live with me from now on. I don't only want to build a future with you but a home, too. What do you think?"

He cupped her face and gave her another gentle kiss, hoping to sway her. It took only a second before Lanie deepened the kiss and wrapped her arms around his neck.

When she eventually pulled back, she looked at him with love in her eyes.

"I'd love that."

Thank you for reading!

If you enjoyed this book, I would sincerely appreciate it if you could take the time to leave a review.

It would mean so much to me!

Ready for the next book?

Stay up to date on Christine Krause's new releases.

Join her mailing list now!

http://newsletter.christinekrause.com

Connect with Christine Krause

Website: www.christinekrause.com
Instagram: @authorchristinekrause
Facebook: @authorchristinekrause

Lightning Source UK Ltd.
Milton Keynes UK
UKHW010746030522
402417UK00002B/319